I0563238

The End of the Treachery

by

H.B. Berlow

The Wichita Chronicles, Book Two

The End of the Treachery

Cover Art by *Tina Lynn Stout*

The Wild Rose Press, Inc.
PO Box 708
Adams Basin, NY 14410-0708
Visit us at www.thewildrosepress.com

Publishing History
First Edition, 2024
Trade Paperback ISBN 978-1-5092-5911-3
Digital ISBN 978-1-5092-5912-0

The Wichita Chronicles, Book Two
Published in the United States of America

Dedication

To Shelia - In one way or another, you have always been a part of my writing.

"Woe to thee that spoilest, and thou wast not spoiled; and dealest treacherously, and they dealt not treacherously with thee! when thou shalt cease to spoil, thou shall be spoiled; and when thou shalt make an end to deal treacherously, they shall deal treacherously with thee."

Isaiah 33:1 KJV

Chapter One

According to the talk around town, Josiah Howard held part ownership of both the De Luxe Barber Shop on East Ninth as well as the Lu Grand Store on North Main. These were two prominent colored businesses of some renown. Rumors even claimed him as a major backer of Butts Motors, likely because several of his friends and associates drove cars from there. Whatever the truth, Alonzo Washington recommended him to me for a domestic matter. My integrity and discretion drew high praise.

Josiah, well over six feet with dark skin yet shiny wavy hair, spoke with a deep baritone voice reminiscent of Paul Robeson singing "Old Man River." The unnerving gaze even affected me. He constantly sized me up and maybe didn't quite come to a conclusion.

He interviewed me for a solid twenty minutes before employing my services. Strangely, however, within three days after hiring me, Mr. Howard handed me a check for five hundred dollars. This was altogether far more than my regular fees and without the benefit of having completed, much less seriously initiated, the investigation outside of a handful of questions to a few of his employees. It seemed my brief inquiries into the activities of his lovely younger wife resulted in her dutiful accompaniment to a show at the Dunbar Theater. There were no further discussions with Mr. Howard after remittance of payment. Alonzo, on the other hand, casually commented that a white man looking into the affairs of a married colored woman turned out to be more detrimental than the nature of those affairs. Mr. Howard knew that as well. I didn't especially enjoy being a pawn in what amounted to a familial game but appreciated the remuneration.

That Alonzo Washington recommended me seemed more like his wife, Althea, pushed him to it as a way of compensation. They needed to repay me in some manner even though getting a crooked cop off Alonzo's back was, to me, a mitzvah. Nevertheless, I would never begrudge anyone else's sense of moral obligation. I took it as a sign of character.

On the flip side, Albert Whitman made an off-hand comment about referring my discretion to a few of his wealthier friends and associates. That was only a tactical brush-off when I encountered him and his daughter in public. As I was in business for myself and hopeful of earning a living wage, economic viability did not necessarily guide my choice of clients. The real importance lay in determining my capabilities, physically, emotionally, and spiritually. For now, I could pay my bills and survive in this new world.

Somewhere around the middle of May, King Mar called me to the back of the Pan American Café while I enjoyed his roast beef sandwich lunch special. At first, I felt annoyed to be taken away from such a delicious sandwich. Nevertheless, I followed dutifully. Before me, in need of a wash, new tires, and a replacement windshield, sat a 1942 Pontiac Torpedo Coupe, a shade of ochre somewhat darker than Sir Pounce, my Manx cat. For that matter, it might have been years of built-up muck and dirt. It was fortunate it wasn't a black-and-white combination, like Lady Mittens, the other feline who lived in my apartment. King Mar had a big smile on his face. I could not determine the reason.

"Nice, huh?" he beamed proudly. I nodded, my eyebrows in the typical position of surprise, trying not to insult a dear friend with a premature comment. Had anyone else observed the scene they would have doubted my detecting skills. "Your birthday's soon, right?" The explanation became clear in a single question.

His generosity knew no bounds. However, there were countless reasons for not wanting to own a car. Limited parking where I lived. Taxes. Maintenance. Although it could prove beneficial in my profession, I had to decline in specific terms that did not come across as personal. He didn't seem to mind.

"No matter," he went on as if I said nothing. "It will be here for you any time you need it. Keys on a hook right inside the kitchen door, huh?"

The gift, for the moment, became a loaner with his intention of becoming permanent.

A week before my birthday, a slight knock on the door did not startle the cats as I poured food into their bowls. Figuring it might be a client, I shut the pocket doors to allow them a quiet repast and myself a peaceful consultation.

The woman, in her late thirties, stood there in a professional gray wool suit. With a solid, almost athletic figure, her reddish blonde hair reminded me of Rita Hayworth. An even stronger shade of red adorned her lips. Instead of a stern businesslike demeanor, she appeared to have been crying, as there were bags under slightly puffy eyes, yet another shade of red. She composed herself once I opened the door.

"Mr. Bergman, I hope I'm not catching you at a bad time." I heard a graciously phrased greeting despite apparent distress. She held herself together passably.

"Not at all. Please come in." I opened the door wider and led her toward the sofa while I sat opposite her. She straightened out her skirt, and then looked up, as though she tried to gather herself back in. She came across as a beautiful woman desperate to not allow that side of her to show.

"My name is Sharon Kaye. My husband and I moved to Wichita back in March."

"Where did you move here from?"

"San Antonio. Before that, Shreveport and then Jacksonville." I raised an eyebrow, which she took for inquisitiveness covered in discretion. She turned out to be correct. "We were independent registered investment advisors. We provided economic planning to people in the communities where we lived. We helped to create portfolios for middle income families. It is lucrative and highly rewarding."

It sounded like a mouthful, but I let it pass.

"You said you 'were' independent advisors?"

She did her best to hold back her emotions, teetering precipitously on the edge of hysteria.

"My husband was…" She stopped, took in a big deep breath, and exhaled slowly. "My husband is dead. The police have concluded it as suicide. I believe it was murder."

"Why do you feel that way?" I asked calmly, an attempt to be soothing in the face of an unspeakable tragedy.

"Martin was not the kind to commit suicide."

"I am quite certain most spouses would say that."

She leaned forward. Perhaps it was an attempt to gain my confidence or convince me of a far more nefarious possibility.

"Our advice has not always resulted in creating expected wealth. Some people have lost their savings for which they blame professionals like my husband and me. Unfortunately, it is practically unavoidable."

"Hence all the moving."

"Precisely."

To me it sounded like desperation, a state of vulnerability. I had familiarity with the Wichita Police Department, their officers and procedures, having been an officer prior to the war. I still had many friends and acquaintances. If they conducted a thorough investigation and determined it a case of suicide, I had no reason to believe otherwise. Nevertheless, I had to assume, for the moment, Mrs. Kaye might have further information that would indicate as such and that her emotions did not guide her. The benefit of the doubt is an initial state of mind. How long it lasts depends entirely upon the client.

"Well, I can certainly look into the matter and determine if there is a path toward resolution. After consulting with the police department, if I decide to take the case, I get twenty-five dollars a day plus expenses, all of which I thoroughly itemize."

"I trust your integrity."

"Where can I reach you?" She gave me her phone number at the Commodore Apartment Hotel, less than half a mile from where I lived. A welcoming tone in her voice wafted in the air after she provided me the address. She stood, extended her hand, which I shook softly, and led her out. I opened the pocket doors and found the cats still ensconced in their bowls, undeterred by my professional meeting. As such, I decided to get a start on this investigation right away. I had the strongest feeling of being in the presence of a grieving woman grasping at straws, but I promised a concerted evaluation.

A warm breezy day in the mid-eighties warranted a brisk walk to police headquarters on William Street. One bullet to the ankle in France made it so the colder weather impacted my damaged foot more than what we experienced now. I still had to be careful about standing too long, walking too much, or dancing excessively. The mile walk became my limit. Hopefully I wouldn't be standing around at the station.

Melvin Bronsky, the desk sergeant on duty, was a man perpetually tired from five children between the ages of seventeen and eight and a wife that had him running chores with about every free moment. Thoughts of retirement hardly scratched the surface of his consciousness; this job stood as the only sanity in his life.

He was let through to Gunny's office. Floyd Gunsaullus currently served in Traffic Safety and had risen through the ranks to be the Division Commander. Undoubtedly one of the best policemen I knew, I had absolute trust in his knowledge and incorruptibility. I believed the feeling was mutual.

"When I see you, I start thinking trouble," he said with a smile. I shook his hand.

"I figured Mendenhall would be sacked out after a night of solving crime." Clarence Mendenhall was head of the newly created Night Detective Squad. After I returned from the war, he encouraged me to rejoin the force and work with him, which fit in with my goal before Pearl Harbor to make detective. What I saw and experienced in Europe made it even more difficult to consider Law and Order as the way of the world.

"You know anything about a Martin Kaye?" I asked Gunny. "You got him pegged as a suicide."

Without hesitation, he picked up the phone and contacted a file clerk. Within three minutes, the folder lay on his desk. He reviewed it briefly.

"They fished his body out of the Arkansas River. A bottle of some cheap hooch was found nearby. Autopsy report indicates either accidental or unintentional act."

"So, no signs of foul play?" I asked.

Gunny looked over the report.

"Contusion on the side of the head indicative of an impact with some of the larger stones found in that area of the river. Coroner does not indicate it as a striking blow due to the angle of impact and nature of the injury." He read a bit more and then looked up at me. "This is about the wife, isn't it?"

"What do you mean?"

"Mrs. Kaye insisted her husband was murdered. We showed her the report, brought her down to the recovery area, explained everything in detail. If Martin Kaye did not kill himself, he might have gotten drunk enough to have a bad accident. She kept telling us he did not even drink. I've seen a lot of these types. If they get down in the dumps, they pick up a bottle."

He had a valid point. Often people close to each other think they know everything about the other. Perhaps this situation arose in which Mr. Kaye became prone to depression or deep despair and Mrs. Kaye just didn't know, or ignored the signs altogether.

"I would think an accidental death would warrant an

7

insurance claim."

"She said they considered his drinking as the primary cause, either by suicide or misadventure."

I paused to consider the predicament she found herself in.

"Gunny, do you know what registered investment advisors are?"

"Well, they're, um, I guess, you know…"

"Yeah. Me neither. Thanks."

By midday, I realized the cats were the only ones who had eaten today. I stopped off at the King's X on Broadway, across the street from the Orpheum Theater. Jennie Palmer was behind the counter as usual, the brightest smile you could find anywhere in Kansas. She might have been a year removed from high school, but she was savvier than most of the sharps walking around.

"Grilled cheese and coffee, please."

"With tomato?"

"Yeah."

"No bacon though."

"Right." I may not have kept kosher, occasionally violating the prohibition of consuming milk and meat by eating a cheeseburger. But I was not inclined to have bacon, ham, or pork and be completely disrespectful. While I had no intention to become a rabbi as my father would have preferred, I still harbored a great deal of respect for my religion.

The food came out in about two minutes, a cup of freshly brewed coffee alongside, and Jennie just stayed there, her elbows holding her in place.

"Jennie, what would you do if you had a lot of money?" I asked in between bites.

"I don't know. Invest it, I guess." I certainly did not

expect that response. For all I knew, she might already have a portfolio of stocks and bonds, just biding her time behind a greasy spoon counter. I could be working for her someday.

"Okay, but how would you invest it?"

"I don't know much about that stuff. I'd probably find someone who was good at it."

"What if their advice didn't work and you, let's say, lost money?" The guy in the overalls eating a club sandwich by the window likely wondered why we had such an intense discussion in the middle of a Tuesday afternoon, at the King's X no less.

"A little money or a lot of money?"

"Well, let's say a lot."

A moment of silence, eyes closed in brief contemplation, and then a look of revelation.

"Shrug my shoulders and move on?"

She had no more answers than I did. The possibility existed that an enraged investor could take his anger out on Martin Kaye. A rock or another foreign object could cause a contusion. I discovered more than simply a grieving wife to make me wonder if the odds were tipped in the favor of murder. I dug a nickel out of my pocket, called Sharon Kaye, and told her I'd take the case.

Chapter Two

Eileen Horowitz surprised me with a knock on my door the next day. We had known each other since high school, dated a couple of times, and unintentionally gave everyone the impression we were on a road toward matrimony. It just very well might have been we didn't care what anyone else thought. Her parents discouraged that notion when they learned of my intentions to become a police officer. Well-educated Jewish males from good families should strive to be doctors or lawyers. To them, I disrespected my parents, my religion, and my God. This despite the fact there were several Jewish members of the Wichita police department. Accordingly, Eileen and I had been close friends ever since.

My thirtieth birthday would be on Tuesday, June 25th, a week from yesterday, and she wanted to help me celebrate it by taking me out on the forthcoming Saturday, the 22nd. I had never given much consideration to turning thirty and had not made any plans nor intended to. All things being equal, it would be pleasant to spend time with Eileen now that we were well past our high school years. She made me promise, however, that I would not opt for dinner at the Pan American. We compromised by agreeing to a light dinner at Candyland on North Broadway where she would treat me to some decadent confections. I begged off from dancing, knowing how her desire to be Ginger Rogers would put a strain on my foot and make me a less-than-suitable Fred Astaire. While I would have preferred to check out *The Blue Dahlia* with Alan Ladd at the Crawford, I acquiesced to *The Harvey Girls* with Judy Garland at the Miller Theater. I decided it would be a good opportunity to drive my gift car.

I looked into Eileen's eyes as we finalized our plans. Part of me wondered why I didn't jump at the chance to be married to her and have a good marriage as my parents had. The way of thinking that carried over from the war, the notion of chaos being in the forefront of everything, gave me an unsettled feeling as though *happiness*, while seemingly easy to attain for many people, would be difficult to hold on to. I gave her a light kiss on the lips as much out of gratitude as for affection. It was soft and sweet and filled with hopeful promise. It made me feel giddy inside.

The gentleman standing on the front stoop as Eileen left made every effort to not appear as though he were eavesdropping or trying to cut in on us. He intentionally looked away, stealing a brief glance only to assure himself when I became available. We were perhaps about the same height, but he had heavy bags under his eyes, and hunched over somewhat, but not in pain or infirmity. Yet his physique still maintained a robustness as though he hadn't given up on life completely. He couldn't have been more than forty but looked almost ready to retire.

"Mr. Bergman?" His voice was barely above a whisper.

"Yes, sir."

"Donald Long. May I have a moment of your time?"

His inflection carried a gentility that belied a deeper strength although I couldn't tell where it might come from. That might be true of most people. Since Eileen adored the cats, they were out and about. Typically, when a prospective client arrived, I shooed them behind the pocket doors. Mr. Long seemed pleased by their presence, a chuckle escaping his lips.

"Well, ain't they a hoot," he commented as a wide smile formed on his face.

The cats approached with caution, circled around the gentleman, and sniffed the air surrounding him to test out his true essence. They were accepting but leery nevertheless.

"The orange fella is Sir Pounce. And that charming tuxedo is Lady Mittens."

"How about that?"

I guided him toward the love seat while I sat in the chair opposite. Without intending to, I looked at him as though he were familiar despite being certain we had never met previously. I rolled his name around in my head like it flew on a roller coaster and then gave sound to my thoughts.

"Donald Long. Don Long? You wouldn't be Slats Long, would you?" Before the war, I remember listening to the Raymond Scott Quintette featuring Wichita's own Slats Long on clarinet. A lot of my musical tastes were sidelined since coming back from Europe and starting this new career. But his name brought me back.

"Well, there ain't much use for a clarinet out at Boeing."

I sensed a story buried somewhere, but I had no reason to dig it out. He was here for another purpose.

"Sorry to hear that." I don't know why I said that.

There might not have been any reason to. I quickly collected myself. "What can I do for you?"

"To tell you the truth, I'm probably stepping out of line here, but it just don't feel right."

"What doesn't?"

"Lady I work with, Arlene Nathan, she got a daughter that probably could use your help, the way I see it. Only Arlene thinks there ain't nothing wrong. May not be my place to say, but it just sticks in my gut is all."

"Why don't you tell me about it?" I sat back to put Don at ease. I could tell Arlene Nathan hadn't put him up to this and likely didn't even know he came here to see me. This would be a second-hand rendition but one stripped of emotion.

"Debra Rose, that's her daughter, graduated high school last year, and then skedaddled for Hollywood just as fast as she could. War was just about coming to a close and all, and she definitely weren't no Rosie the Riveter type. She'd have been all thumbs out there. She's a pretty gal who'd done some plays with the Drama Club. Now, my opinion don't count for all that much in spite of my background. But she's nowhere nearly as pretty as Deanna Durbin and nothing to write home about as an actress."

"Small town girl wants to make it big in pictures, huh?"

"Exactly. Arlene didn't say nothing, didn't stop her, figured she'd be out on her own someday anyway. Might as well let her get her feet wet now. Kinda made sense. The fledgling has to fly eventually, right? Well, she comes back in a huff about a month ago, told her mom she made a big mistake, a real big mistake, but you know, all's well that ends well. You know?"

Apparently, it hadn't because Slats Long took those once elegant hands that travelled silkily up and down a licorice stick and wringed them back and forth. It looked like he was about to break a knuckle and tear a finger right off. He looked down as though the answer to the mystery lay somewhere on my rug. All he found were two cats looking up at him in amazement.

"What happened?"

"She disappeared. Plum gone. Not like when she went to California."

"Take anything with her?"

"No, sir. Just up and vanished. Here one day, gone the next."

Just two months ago I spent a considerable amount of time looking for two other missing people. Caroline Whitman and Alonzo Washington were both caught up in issues very much over their respective heads. Unless someone decides to leave of their own accord for greener pastures, my impression was that missing folks typically ran away from an element too powerful to control.

"Don, tell me what you think." I had a momentary thought to call him Slats, but I figured segueing into the aircraft industry from swing music might have been a good enough reason to avoid an old moniker. Besides, it was respectful to address him as he introduced himself.

"I don't rightly know. Last year, she had stars in her eyes. This time, it could be just about anything. Since she didn't talk much about it, I can't really figure."

"Any man in her life, a boyfriend of some sort?"

"Not that I know of."

"How about someone older? Maybe a theater manager or a talent agent?"

He shook his head negatively.

If I dug, I could find a deep ache to this story, one not about a spoiled rich girl or a down-and-out colored man. A story about emptiness that longed for fulfillment. This came across like a tragedy brewing, one that I hoped could be avoided.

"Well, I can't just go and take on a case on your say so. You understand that."

"Yes, I do, Mr. Bergman. Maybe you could come with me and talk to Arlene, um, Mrs. Nathan? I got a car out front."

I caught him as he referred to the mother more personally but didn't let on that I had. He was a man with a deep sense of compassion. It seemed he had transitioned from music to another passion.

Considering the fact the cats were relatively happy, I motioned for Mr. Long to lead the way. He made his way slowly over to Hydraulic and took George Washington Boulevard south toward Plainview, the housing built for aircraft workers during the war. They were functional but certainly nothing in terms of elegance or style. The Albert Whitmans of the world likely didn't even know such neighborhoods existed. Don turned off East Ross Parkway and then down a dead-end street called Whitney Lane. The houses all looked the same. They had a simple slab that passed for a front porch. Some front doors had screen doors as well; some did not. The rectangular box of a house likely had two bedrooms and one bathroom, a small kitchen, and a front room barely enough to hold a couple of chairs. No one had a garage. For that matter, there weren't too many cars around. The aircraft industry still thrived after the war, and their employees lived like refugees.

The influx of aircraft workers during the war

expanded the population of Wichita. There had still been plenty of work afterward which created a shortage of both housing and basic goods and supplies. I found myself quite lucky to get my apartment at 730 North Market in the fall of 1945. The city did not build neighborhoods like Plainview with the expectation of permanence. Consequently, they had the appearance of imminent decay. Perhaps the residents did as well.

Mrs. Nathan's house had a screen door and a canopy over the concrete slab on which there were two pots of flowers in desperate need of water, if that would even help. What little grass popped up wouldn't need mowing for quite some time, if at all. The heat seemed to resonate off the building. Everything looked dry and parched. I saw barely anything that gave the impression of human life within.

Don tapped lightly on the screen door. Shortly, the front door opened. Arlene Nathan did not look that much older than me. Perhaps the wear and tear of life had sucked out whatever beauty she once had. She looked like someone who was always tired for one reason or another, hardly able to dredge up a smile or make her eyes wide with excitement. Such an effort would almost be painful. I had seen that look in the faces of soldiers who had been through repeated battles. In one regard, they were already dead. Their bodies just weren't aware.

She looked at me inquisitively and then at Don. I could tell she wanted to be upset with him but had the good sense and manners not to do so publicly. Her restraint likely took all the energy she had.

"Arlene, this is Mr. Bergman. He's a private detective."

"Sorry Don brought you all the way here, Mr.

Bergman. But what I've got is nothing more than a wild impetuous daughter that thinks there is some kind of shortcut to life." Her voice had the graciousness and charm of a Southern belle.

"Well, maybe there is, Mrs. Nathan. Maybe your daughter actually found it."

She nodded her head, the smile forced.

"I don't think so," she said forlornly.

She walked away from the screen door but kept the main door open.

Don beckoned me to follow him.

Arlene Nathan had sat down in one of the two chairs in an area that passed for a parlor. She picked up a washcloth or doily she crocheted and continued to work on it. It did not appear to be much of anything. The nervous energy had to go somewhere.

Don encouraged me to sit down opposite her while he stood unobtrusively behind us.

"Why don't you tell me what you think happened? Maybe there is no reason for me to be here. Then again, I might be able to help."

She continued to crochet, a regular rhythm that created further rows that would become a sweater or a blanket. Maybe it would eventually be a long row of a pretty looking nothing. She looked down at her work even though she could have done it blindfolded. She looked at me, I assumed, like I was a truth she could not bear to face, a real and tangible thing from this world that she did not want to be reminded of.

"I had Debra Rose when I was her age, just out of high school. The father of the boy sent him away to military school in South Carolina, sort of like his punishment for consorting with me. Jimmy Nathan came along, a decent man who offered to marry me and be a father to my child. We didn't have much, Mr. Bergman. Heck, we didn't have anything. But somehow, we got by. And we laughed a lot." She barely smiled at a memory that had blown away like a cloud in a Kansas wind. "Of course, Debra Rose was a little headstrong and didn't much see things the same way. Jimmy joined up in '42, got sent over to Africa, died somewhere there."

"Tunisia," Don chimed in. "Battle of Kasserine Pass. February 1943."

"I worked at Boeing when I met Don. He's been looking out for us since."

"It ain't nothing, Arlene."

I wondered why people weren't allowed to be happy. Perhaps too many traumas from the past make the path forward covered in ash. The Talmud tells us "*He who has been bitten by a snake is scared of a rope.*" Probably as likely true of me as well. Then again, each of us had our own demons, the point being to face them and overcome them and use whatever tools were at our disposal. That was how we survived. Arlene Nathan drowned in her demons.

"When she come back, I figured the stars in her eyes faded," she continued. "She acted awful quiet and mopey. Like a balloon had popped and scared her before she realized it was just a balloon. I tried to get her a job out at Boeing, and Don here said they was looking for checkers at the Dillons nearby. If she, you know, had a job and made her own money that might give her a sense of herself. She needed something that I couldn't give her."

"When did she go missing?"

"Last Thursday. I come back from work, and she

was gone. Didn't know what to think. Talked with Don about it late Friday. He got all excited more than I did."

"You didn't?" I tried not to sound judgmental. You never know if you are successful or not. She just nodded her head.

"I figured she got some kind of itch again to go roaming."

"Tell him about the guy," Don said somewhat mysteriously.

"I seen a guy, heavy set, greasy hair and moustache, a couple of times. Once down the end of the street and once as I pulled in to the parking lot at work."

"When was this?" I asked.

"Tuesday and Wednesday of last week."

"Did he ever approach you or Debra Rose?"

She shook her head but gave me nothing further.

"Could that be something, Mr. Bergman?" Don asked excitedly.

"Could be," I responded to him without putting too much weight on it, and then turned toward her. "There is too much about this that doesn't seem right, Mrs. Nathan. I'd like to take a couple of days to investigate this a little more."

"Mr. Bergman, I don't have no money to pay you for this. We barely get by."

Donald Long stepped forward, as if Slats came alive again, about to take a solo. "Don't you worry about nothing, Arlene."

She bowed her head and returned to the crochet.

Donald Long took me by the arm and guided me out of the house. He had all the look of a father, maybe even a grandfather, a stern and solemn figure who would charge headlong into battle. His head bowed at first, but he lifted it with the pride and dignity of a scholar.

"You do whatever you need to, Mr. Bergman. And don't worry nothing about payment. Whatever is going on ain't right. Debra Rose was all set about staying after what went on out there."

"What did go on out there, Mr. Long?" Now I sounded like the concerned parent.

"She never said, other than she made a big mistake."

Sadly, in my experience, our past mistakes had a way of catching up to us.

Chapter Three

Martin and Sharon Kaye had a second-floor office in a building across from Union Station. The main floor had a For Lease sign attached; various other businesses took up the rest of the space on the third and fourth floors. One door with a glass panel in need of cleaning advertised a lawyer who I thought had been disbarred. A woman in her seventies offered services as a travel agent. A certified public accountant held a quiet back office. The painted sign on the smoked glass door on the second floor simply read KAYE INVESTMENTS. Mrs. Kaye had provided me with the keys, but given what I found inside, it might as well have been left unlocked.

I encountered a desk with a comfortable-looking leather chair behind it but a sturdy and rugged wooden chair without any padding or cushion in front. A wooden filing cabinet, old and used with several scratches; a smaller table and chair near the window overlooked Douglas Avenue that appeared more suited to a café; and graphs in black ink pinned to the walls. A quick perusal led me to believe they were an indication of rates of return on different investments, although I lacked the knowledge of the field to make a firm determination. It had an impressive look to a layman. Whether any substance lay behind it was still uncertain.

It struck me I could find nothing remotely personal about the place, something to indicate the dispositions of

Martin or Sharon Kaye. No photographs or memorabilia of their various prior places of residence. Similarly, outside of the graphs pinned to the walls, the place lacked any professional enhancements that one would typically find in, let's say, a bank manager's office. Certifications, diplomas, professional photos with well-known individuals. If I were to have acquired some money and wanted to build a portfolio, this would be the last place I would come. Perhaps that bordered on judgmental or completely wrong based on not being acquainted with this field. But businesses are supposed to create an air of importance and knowledge that would result in a healthy respect. This looked like a generic room that could have housed a bookkeeper, an appraiser, or even a private detective.

I looked through the desk drawers and found pencils and paper clips and receipt books, mostly standard office supplies. The contents of the file cabinet included a handful of folders with names of residents from Wichita, Belle Plaine, Newton, Augusta, and El Dorado. A standard form in each of them contained basic and primary information: name, address, date of birth, annual household income. I assumed these were recent clients. Perhaps an interview with some of them might lead me somewhere. I would consider that as a possible venue for investigation, intending to maintain their privacy as well as that of Sharon Kaye. In all, I collected a lot of general information but nothing substantive to either define the Kayes themselves or Martin's motivations.

I found Richie Mayer's hack parked at his usual spot down on Douglas between Broadway and Market. His chronic asthma impacted just about every aspect of his life, yet he still found a way to push through it. To me, he always acted like he had to catch up to life. He mistook the Jewish name "Hirsch" as a nickname for Harold. The kid was too pleasant to contradict. Even with King Mar's generous gift, I knew I needed to throw some consideration in Richie's direction. He made good greenbacks off me in the past few months.

"Where to, Hirsch?"

"South Riverside Park."

I likely caught him off guard by the request. Usually, I had him take me to businesses or homes of clients. A pleasant afternoon stroll in the park might not be too usual for a private detective.

Gunny had told me specifically where they found Martin Kaye's body. Since the police ruled the death as accidental or possible suicide, the area was not a crime scene and blocked off in any fashion. Richie pulled over as close to the curb on Nims Drive as possible while I walked down the pathway along the Arkansas River. Kaye's car still sat parked at the office building on Douglas. That meant he would have had to walk anywhere from a mile and a half to two miles, presumably in a drunken stupor, to have made his way to this location. Perhaps he didn't start his imbibing until he got to a cozy spot on the riverbank. A stretch of the imagination, for sure. I had trouble picturing either a despondent suicide or an intoxicated accident in this manner. Every possibility existed he could have been abducted by a perpetrator and brought to this quiet location to be killed. But by who? The insinuation of a disgruntled client indicated a crime of passion, one of emotion rather than deliberation. A meeting in the office followed by a heated argument that eventually led to an impulsive act. Anything like that made sense. I found a scene in the park incomprehensible.

When I completed an uninspired perusal of the area, Richie drove me over to the Commodore Apartments. I asked him to wait. Sharon Kaye answered after a brief polite knock on her door. This time, she appeared less like a grieving widow and more like a determined executive. She had a brusque and quick manner. Her wardrobe ran toward deep navy with a sparkly brooch, almost a prism. That same deep red lipstick remained, but the eyes were decorated by much more than tears.

"Have you made any determination yet, Mr. Bergman?"

"Only that I am unwilling to accept the police report without further investigation."

"Good." Her voice did not contain any sense of pleasure that I started to see things her way. I took it as simply a comment made to move the conversation forward.

"Based on your theory of a disgruntled client, I will need your permission to review the files in your office. I would like to be able to interview some folks and get a general assessment of their opinions."

"Is that necessary?" The question was not as concerning as the slow and distinct way she asked it. The runaway train started slowing in the station.

"Yes. One of those folks may have some knowledge in this matter, assuming they are not the actual killer."

She looked at me and then, apparently, over my shoulder, before she looked back at me again. She still didn't respond.

"Otherwise, we will have no recourse but to accept the police report as a closed matter."

"They are at your complete disposal." She rose,

shook my hand, and escorted me out. I wondered if this was the same woman who had hired me. With this air of nonchalance, she acted as though I intruded on something of vastly greater importance, a fly buzzing around at an outdoor cocktail party. Perhaps the grieving had ended. To each his own.

As Richie drove me back to my apartment, I asked him, "If you had a family member who was killed, wouldn't you do everything possible to find the killer?"

"Well, sure. Ain't that happening, Hirsch?"

Sadly, I couldn't answer his question.

My father had invited me over to dinner this Thursday evening. He figured I might have an actual social event to celebrate my birthday. I shaved and put on a clean shirt, fed the cats, and then went down to the Pan American to retrieve the car and drive to my father's house on South Kansas Street just off Douglas Avenue. Being relatively close to Hebrew Congregation of Wichita, my father could regularly attend services. He was much more than a jewelry and watch repairman. No one could impugn his integrity. He exhibited sincerity of the highest order. The entire congregation knew this to be true, not just his devoted son. I hoped to have a thimble's worth of his character.

As I entered his house, I respectfully put on a yarmulke. In his presence, I adhered to all the rites of a Jew. My Hebrew was strong. My Yiddish, suspect. I had sufficient knowledge to become a rabbi, which would have pleased my father to no end. I just did not have enough faith after the horrors of war to walk blindly into a maelstrom. He accepted my decision graciously but with mostly silent misgivings. His faith allowed him to believe I would find the path.

The pot roast was exquisitely tender, and the carrots and potatoes had the flavors of black pepper and herbs. To my surprise, my father even baked a challah. We said a prayer over the braid and lit candles. A kind of breathlessness overtook me when I thought how much I missed my mother, who had passed shortly after I enlisted. She would have been proud of the two of us. Her presence warmed this house as it had throughout my childhood and lingered like a soft finger wrapped in velvet tracing the smile on my face.

"You have plans for your birthday?" my father inquired.

"Dinner and a movie with Eileen Horowitz."

"Ah, lovely girl. I had hopes for the two of you."

"Her parents didn't want a cop for a son-in-law."

"Understandable. It was not exactly your mother's and mine first choice either." My father would not elaborate of his feelings of my original choice of profession. He simply stated an opinion and left it at that. "You're working?" By that, he meant what clients I might have.

"Missing girl."

"Tell me."

This had become a typical conversation. He wished to know the basics of the cases I worked without lurid details. He fully understood how this aspect of my life allowed me to come to terms with human beings and the lives we led. He could appreciate my need to reconcile what I experienced in the war with the traditions of my faith. His questioning almost Socratic in nature. I went into detail about Debra Rose Nathan, her mother, and the former jazz musician who, in essence, became their benefactor. My father came from the Old Country and looked at things from a completely different perspective. He had neither law enforcement nor military experience but held an enlightened perception of the world, the kind of awareness you could sense deep in your gut. In some fashion, this sort of repartee also bonded us despite our philosophical differences.

"She's running away from something," I commented.

"True. But is that something here in Wichita or over there in Hollywood?"

The angle at which a thing is viewed determines the direction it is both coming from and going to. Originally, Debra Rose became a star struck gal from Kansas who sought out the bright lights. When she returned, she travelled in haste and desperation. By all rights, she should have been comfortable back with her mother. Yet something spooked her enough to disappear again. Discomfort and boredom sent her away the first time. I sensed a greater concern caused this departure. Something perhaps even darker.

We sat in the parlor after cleaning up the dishes from dinner, a small lamp the only light in the room. It gave off a glow of warmth, the kind an infant feels in its mother's arms. This place had always been safe to me, almost a blessing.

"I don't mean to pry, Harold," my father said in a low voice, "nor push you in any direction. But have you considered the possibility of marriage?"

At first, I thought I would hear again his wishes that I become a rabbi again. This commentary, however, came as a surprise. I used my analytical mind and quickly tried to determine the impetus behind the comment. Perhaps, as he got older, he hoped to become a grandfather. Then, I considered there weren't too many married private detectives around. By entering matrimony, a good wife, someone like Eileen, would encourage me into a more stable occupation, one that would not have put me in jeopardy or risk of losing my life.

Certainly, all that instantaneous thought was mere speculation. I would never have asked my dad why he asked what he did. That would have been disrespectful. In the past, since my return from the war, I had done my best to explain how it felt to be caught in a whirlwind of uncertainty. My foot injury had not incapacitated me, but it had impacted everything from running and walking to dancing. The atrocities I encountered as a soldier were far worse than any crimes I investigated as a police officer. Previously, my path in life lay on a road of certainty. Now, I had doubts. This career of investigation became my way of attempting to figure things out. If I ever could.

I placed my hand gently on my father's and looked at him directly and honestly.

"Someday, Pop."

He was satisfied enough with the answer.

On the way home, I stopped by the Kayes' office, took the folders from the filing cabinet, and put them in a worn heavy canvas satchel I found there. Now that I had her permission to review the files, it would make this research easier. I needed to understand their business, what they did, and how they did it. After that, I could attempt to interview some of their clients. I doubted that a farmer up in Newton would resort to murder, but you could never tell. Cain did okay until he got annoyed with his brother.

I dropped off the car at the Pan American. King Mar saw me put the keys back on the hook in the kitchen and asked me how it ran. I told him it worked well and even impressed my father. That pleased him. My father's approval might mean my full acceptance of this gift. I walked back up Market Street with a satchel like a regular old businessman. There was an oddly natural aspect in a way I never previously considered. Maybe my father's comment impacted me after all. Then again, I knew I wasn't ready to sit in an office for eight hours a day either.

Lady Mittens greeted me as I entered the apartment. Typically, she would be lying somewhere peacefully, and Sir Pounce would mew to beat the band. They were both likely going to be pleased that I would be up for a while, sitting on a chair in the parlor with a bunch of files on the coffee table. Since they slept most of the day, the opportunity to be playful was a rarity. Unfortunately for them, digging into financial matters of which I knew very little made me feel like a student back at Wichita High School East all over again. A former police officer and war veteran found himself saddled with homework.

Chapter Four

I woke up on my sofa in a daze, with crusty bits in the corner of my eyes and a couple of the folders open with papers everywhere. I didn't recall them falling to the floor or any disruption by my feline roommates. Apparently, I dozed off while I tried to translate the complex data relating to various client accounts. The uncertainty of what the documents contained made me completely weary. Sir Pounce looked up at me from down at my feet while Lady Mittens sat distinctively in the kitchen in front of the drawer that held the cat food cans. Before seeing to their needs, the thought occurred to me that others, less intellectually inclined, would have been even more confused. Either they had great faith in Sharon and Martin Kaye or something was amiss.

As I stumbled to the kitchen to take care of the feline culinary needs, I realized this was Friday and I needed to get some deep research done before tomorrow night's outing with Eileen. Also, I considered the possibility of a trip to Los Angeles to determine what Debra Rose Nathan had been up to while on her sojourn. While there was no degree of excessive mewing, the cats seemed quite content with their morning meal. I, on the other hand, made do with cereal. Time stood at my back and exerted its influence.

There were two clients in Wichita that seemed worthy of an interview. It would save me the trouble of a trip all the way out to El Dorado, at least an hour's drive each way. Horatio Frazier, a long-time mechanic, had a small house just east of Lincoln and Broadway. The car in the driveway exhibited a spit-shine polish in stark contrast to the weeds that took up residence in the front lawn. You could tell where his main interests landed.

I found him to be a likeable sort in his mid-fifties. He wore overalls with a handkerchief in his back pocket and a solid chaw of tobacco in his mouth. The squint of his eyes gave an indication of uncertainty, as though he perpetually tried to figure out the deeper mysteries of life. Over all, he came across as a hard-working sort, not prone to vacations or excessive spending. He gave a good spit before he invited me in.

"Mrs. Kaye doesn't accept the police report and believes her husband was killed," I said bluntly. I didn't think I could spook him or get him to confess. I wasn't even sure if he should be considered a suspect although I suppose, based on Mrs. Kaye's theory, anyone might have been. In this case, I had more of a need to know how he acted as a client. Anything else I determined would be a bonus.

"You don't say," he simply responded as his head nodded slightly. He picked up a dirty coffee cup and gave another good spit. I couldn't tell if he was disinterested, disbelieving, or dishonest.

"What kind of investments did you have with them?"

"Well, you know, Mr. Bergman, I don't rightly know." I sat up in surprise. "That kind of stuff is way over my head. It all sounded pretty good. Now, you want to talk about rebuilding a carburetor or fixing a fuel pump, I'm your man."

For a moment, I acted like a character in a Daffy Duck cartoon. Here I stood talking with a man about his hard-earned money, and he acted as if it didn't concern him in the least. He might have been aloof, secretly rich, or hiding a mental malady.

"So, you never inquired about the investments?"

"Of course, I did. Any sensible man would. But then Mr. Kaye pulls out graphs and points to the charts on his office wall and started in on Return on Investment, Liquidation, Capital Investiture, and a whole lot of other big words that flew over my head like a flock of Canadian geese on the way to Havana. He sounded smart enough, smiled a lot, and indicated I could wind up with a six to eight percent return within six months. The way he made it sound I figured that was okay."

"Have you gotten any of your money back, now that he's passed away?"

"Mrs. Kaye says the money's all tied up in probate. Them lawyers." Another spit followed the comment.

He mentioned that Sharon Kaye had contacted him the day after Martin's death, guaranteed him that she would ensure the process moved as quickly as the law allowed. Satisfied with those assurances, he hadn't given the money a second thought until I visited. He likely wouldn't think of it any further until someone else brought up the matter. I figured him to be the kind of guy who would have a socket wrench or tire iron in his hand right up until he died. The notion of making more money than he needed for his living expenses was practically foreign to him. I thanked him for his time.

Reginald Kraft, on the other hand, showed a bit more concern about his investment. He had also been advised by Sharon Kaye of the probate issue on the same day. He appeared to be in his mid to late sixties, a very proud-looking man who wore a vest, shirt and tie, pressed pants, and cordovan wingtip shoes. His forty years as a tailor showed in both his wardrobe and demeanor. He had an air of fastidiousness about him.

He indicated he asked specific questions of Martin Kaye, things he had researched before he went to the office as a way of not getting bamboozled. Satisfied with the answers, he was more impressed with the confidence exuded by Mr. Kaye, especially in this post-war period. He would read the papers daily and follow along with the financial news he found. He kept meticulous track of his investments but received fewer communications from either of the Kayes as days and weeks passed. He thought nothing of it at the time, given the various changes in the stock market.

"I understand how these things work, Mr. Bergman. Investments, probate, legal, and financial matters whose wheels move far too slowly for most of us who do not have the patience nor understanding." I caught a hint of disappointment and frustration in his voice, but he appeared too proud to allow it to come out fully, certainly not for my sake. When he asked me to look into his claim, I simply nodded because I didn't have the heart to tell him he really needed a lawyer. That was well beyond my purview.

I determined by the two visits these were small time investors, no more than five thousand dollars each, with no exquisitely lavish promises in terms of specific numbers. The same graphs and charts I saw on the walls were either tools or fancy wallpaper, enough to give the impression of financial acumen on the part of the Kayes. Given Sharon Kaye's sincerity, I dismissed the notion of an elaborate scam especially given my employment by those who would have perpetrated it. Yet I still could not deeply consider an angry investor taking out some measure of revenge. That would be more in line with a Bette Davis melodrama. If it were murder, there had to be another and separate motive. This would take some looking into Martin and Sharon Kaye's background. It would take Carla Duggan.

My favorite librarian at the Wichita Carnegie Library was a feisty redhead, often flighty in nature, but who had more knowledge in her pinkie than some of the professors at Wichita University. I had to guess her to be in her forties because she would never tell me the truth. Her life story was a series of anecdotes you would need to piece together for yourself. Far too smart to be only in her twenties and too glamorous to be all the way to sixty, in the end, that didn't matter. She had refreshing effervescence and impeccable knowledge. That meant far more to me.

She walked up the steps just outside the library, likely having returned from lunch, when she saw me get out of the car. She began laughing.

"What in the name of Job is so funny?" I asked demurely.

"You drive a car the same color as your cat. Is that the Sir Pounce-mobile?" She continued laughing as broadly as Martha Raye while I escorted her to the front door. As we entered, she immediately went into her quiet librarian mode. I followed her to the main desk.

"What do you know about personal investment counselors?" I asked bluntly.

"I lump them in with bankers, lawyers, and car salesmen. All crooks."

"I'm trying to track down the dealings of a couple who moved here from San Antonio. Before that, they were in Shreveport and Jacksonville. Anything related to shady financial dealings or criminal cases against Martin and Sharon Kaye."

"Martin Kaye?" Her eyes bugged out in a fashion I had never seen. "The guy who died?"

"Yeah. Why?"

"He came in here about a month ago."

"What did he want?"

"Information about estate planning and wills. I told him we had some books, but he would be better off going to a lawyer. Then I mentioned he looked too young to be planning that kind of stuff."

"Did he say anything to that?"

"Kinda like, you'll never know when life will take a funny turn. Personally, I don't figure dying is all that funny."

Carla indicated it would take a couple of days to scour three different sets of newspapers that went back six months to a year. She asked me to come back by next Tuesday. I told her I might be out of town but didn't respond when she asked if it were a vacation. Besides, she should have known better.

Donald Long had a shabby apartment off Hillside just south of Pawnee. There were no grocery marts or even churches nearby. Just a liquor store and a couple of rundown buildings that may or may not have contained businesses. I heard music before I knocked on the door. Even though he'd left the jazz scene, the music stays in your blood. Once a musician, always a music lover. The music stopped and the door opened. I saw nothing on the walls, no artwork or photos. The furniture had no decorative slipcovers or quaint throw pillows. A pile of magazines stood stacked next to a chair, likely his favorite. A table held a radio and a record player. A small collection of records sat on the shelf below.

The man formerly known as Slats invited me in graciously and offered me a seat. As I looked around, I had a hard time believing him to be someone willing to foot the expenses of a private investigator for a woman he clearly had a tender fondness for. It occurred to me we all make sacrifices of one kind or another.

"Mr. Long, I need to know everything you know about Debra Rose's time in Los Angeles. Where she lived. Friends or acquaintances. Did she work? It will help determine where she could be now."

He scratched his head for quite some time. I could tell he strained to offer a comment that would result in a hopeful resolution. What he didn't know was that any scrap could be a starting point.

"Well, I don't rightly know about friends. She never mentioned any gals or guys. There was a fella, a photographer named, um, Brooks Mellon. Met her in clothing store. Took quite an interest in her. Said she had good cheekbones. Whatever that's supposed to mean."

"Was it legit?"

"As far as I know. She sent a few letters to Arlene…her mom early on, but then they just plain stopped coming. Let me see if I got one here."

He got up and made his way to the cramped kitchen. I did not follow. I heard him while he opened and closed several drawers until an "aha" came from that room. He handed it to me and sat back down.

The letter was typical for a young girl. All giddy and happy to be where she thought she wanted to be.

Mentioning Brooks Mellon and how he had a way to get her into the pictures, but not elaborating how with any details. Likely the same line he had given to countless starry-eyed gals who made the bold venture of traveling west. I told Don the return address was a good place to start. I reiterated the expense of flying out there, even for a brief time.

"Mr. Bergman," he started quietly but firmly, "I had a good career, made some good money, and decided to move on with my life. What you see here might not be much. What I value the most is my friendship with Arlene. Knowing her as I do, she is tied up in knots inside. No, we need to find Debra Rose. That right there is the end of it."

He made no mention of money. The man was too proud. I had forgotten how valuable that could be.

Chapter Five

Bradley Wolrebinski, a Polish Jew who wrote lurid crime fiction under the name R.C. Donnelly, lived in a rather stately house on Park Place with his artist wife, Svetlana Halonen who was a half-Russian and half-Finnish painter and sculptor. I had met them at various social functions and temple events before I enlisted. They were gregarious, brash, and colorful. The perfect embodiment of the artistic temperament. Visiting them, however, always amounted to a grab bag. I never knew which of the two of them would be more eccentric. It made for entertaining encounters.

Bradley answered the door at eleven a.m. on that Saturday morning, with an aggrieved look. Likely, I should have waited until considerably after noon, given there was always a party of a Friday evening that would have lasted well until the wee hours of the morning and included quite a bit of drinking. I learned this to be the life of artists. However, he gave me a bear hug on the front porch when he saw me and then dragged me inside.

"Svetlana, coffee," he yelled. "And eggs."

She stuck her head out from the kitchen, dressed in a smock with paint stains.

"I was about to tell you to get it yourself. But with our dear Harold here to visit, I will bring you coffee. Eggs you make yourself."

He waved her off, and she returned to the kitchen.

Wichita had its own version of Burns and Allen.

"What brings you here today?"

"Crime."

"My favorite subject."

In our typical manner, one probably preferred by him, I leaned forward in a conspiratorial manner. Bradley always assumed my jobs were replete with deep intrigue. Philandering spouses and divorces held no interest for him outside of plots for his novels.

"A young girl, fresh out of high school, goes to Hollywood to find fame. Several months later, she returns and is largely secretive about what went on. A few weeks after her return, she disappears."

Bradley sat up straight, hand stroking his chin, and just about to make a declaration when Svetlana walked in with a tray that contained two cups and saucers. She gracefully handed me mine and then clumsily placed her husband's down on the small table in front of him. She gave him a smirk and me a pat on the head before she departed.

"You've got two issues, yes?" he said.

"I've got a missing girl."

"Ah, but the first is starry-eyed girl returns to home in secrecy after willingly going to California. The other is same girl disappears with no prior declaration or viable intention." He had a point. The Los Angeles experience may or may not have had anything to do with her current disappearance. "Pornography," he blurted out, more of a concept than a word.

"What?"

"If you had read my books, you'd know what I am talking about. Do you know how many countless young girls from all over the country flock to Dreamland in hopes of a movie career?"

"Countless?"

"Exactly. And then some. Too many to appear in movies but just enough to get their photos taken for smut magazines. And what happens to them?"

"Tell me."

"Some make it a career. Some become hooked on drugs and turn to prostitution. And some have the good sense to go back home and give up on their dreams before it winds up being too late." In the past, any discussions with Bradley also came with a story about the extensive research he had done. While his works were largely pulp paperbacks, he had pride as a writer to make every effort to produce a quality product. With a background just secretive enough, an allure added to his larger-than-life persona. Even I had no real inkling of an accurate biography of him.

All Bradley's comments made sense for the first part. Her being missing now was still an uncertainty. I considered the necessity of a trip to Los Angeles to track down a smut photographer. First, however, my evening with Eileen.

I got back to my apartment in time to help my landlady, Constance Hanover, carry in groceries to her own flat. She gave me a loaf of some baked goods, knowing that I did not keep kosher and would not be bothered by the ingredients. I showered, shaved, and put on a clean shirt and tie. I hadn't planned to get overly dressed up, but I didn't want Eileen to think this was not important to me. On the contrary, the company held for more significance than the occasion.

I fed the cats, who then scurried off, obviously aware they would be by themselves for the evening.

While I realized Eileen had invited me, I had no interest in it being Sadie Hawkins Day. So, I went on down to the Pan American, grabbed the car key off the hook in the kitchen, and headed over to her apartment. Candyland was just down the block from the Miller on Broadway. We parked nearby and ambled about on this pleasant June evening. Fortunately, my foot held up for it.

A couple of burgers and French fries became my birthday dinner. Eileen had a yen for Candyland's cream puffs. I had my heart set on an éclair, but I acquiesced. We reminisced about our childhood, high school, the first time she saw me with a yarmulke in temple for the High Holidays when we were just kids, and the pride she displayed at my Bar Mitzvah. The only item missing was a malted milkshake and two straws while our foreheads came imminently close. I acted giddy and young, for a moment not thinking about what it meant to be a policeman or a soldier or a private detective. Just a guy with a big smile on my face. The pleasantries were worthwhile, even necessary. Yet I still had a feeling of yearning for a greater truth that I knew to be hidden from me and that I would have to find by myself.

We sank into our seats at the Miller, each with a bag of popcorn, and saw a short film before Judy Garland, John Hodiak, Ray Bolger, and Angela Lansbury took the screen. It turned out to be a big and colorful movie, very nostalgic, and just the thing to take my mind off the countless girls who flocked to Dreamland in hopes of a movie career. We came out of the theater singing "On the Atchison, Topeka, and the Santa Fe" and were impressed that a major Hollywood musical referenced trains in Kansas.

There must have been a less-than-jovial look on my face because Eileen reached out and touched my cheek softly. She referenced the old speakeasy in the basement of the Broadview. My mood turned this festive occasion rather gray.

I'm not much of a drinker, but the bartender had a reputation for quality and precision. I ordered a Manhattan while Eileen got a Mary Pickford. We sat in silence while the waiter brought us our drinks. We each took a sip. The tension needed to be broken otherwise the evening would be lost.

"Eileen, I have had such a great time with you. I can't remember when I've enjoyed myself this much."

"Probably back in high school," she said somberly. I looked at her perplexed. "Harold, you became a policeman, and a very good one, and then a soldier. I'm sure you saw things there and did things that are just too horrific to talk about. But you have got to give yourself a break."

"From what?" I tried not to sound incredulous. More shocking to me were her powers of perception. She would have made a pretty good detective herself.

"Your enlisting had nothing to do with your mother's passing."

That thought crept in the back of my mind for almost a year now, and it wasn't a subject I talked about with anyone, not even my father. Perhaps that was the one significant thing that made me have both doubt and regrets. All this time I saddled myself with concerns over the horrors of the war, the boys that didn't come back and those who did with far worse ailments than my gimpy foot. After Pearl Harbor, I had no compunction about leaving the police department for the greater good.

I just had never given any consideration to how that decision impacted my parents, both their spiritual well-being and their physical.

At the same time, I realized how much I missed my mother and saw how many of her qualities were in Eileen. She had an intelligence based on deep inner reflection as well as the kind of empathy found in so few people. My father's words echoed in my head, and I started to look upon Eileen as more than just "that gal from high school." It had taken me that long to realize how truly special she was.

"What is it you're looking for, Eileen?"

"If you think I'm going to be shy and coy, Harold Bergman, you don't know me well." We smiled together. "I want what my parents have."

"What exactly is that?"

"A deep and abiding love. A commitment to family. A joy for living. And following Adonai's laws. I want a husband who wants the same."

I smiled broadly at her, thinking that, deep down, I wanted the same, and knowing her well, she would be a wonderful partner for life. Then, like a switch that flipped, I considered how I had been placed in the path of people looking for others who were meaningful to them. I did not necessarily choose this; I was the one chosen. With her hand reaching across the table for mine, I felt her choose me as well.

"You know it is likely I have loved you since we were little kids," I said unashamedly. "That hasn't changed. The world around us has. I have these…things I need to do. Kind of like packing up an old trunk and putting it into storage. Eventually, it won't be necessary, but right now this is what I need to do."

"I haven't considered anyone else that would fill the bill like you."

"What about Ruben Bishkoff?" I said dead seriously.

"He had bad breath," she responded.

We laughed and all was right with the world.

We got back to her apartment close to midnight. We sat in the car, stared ahead, and said nothing for a long time.

"I think I need to go to California. It might hold the answers to where a missing girl might be."

She nodded.

"Eileen, I…"

She put a finger over my lips, then leaned in and kissed me more passionately than I had ever experienced before.

I could smell her face powder and her perfume and her absolute feminine beauty. I couldn't be sure if it was my heart or hers I could hear beating. I walked her to the front door, but then turned when she entered and got back into my car without looking back. That would be something I would be working on as I moved forward.

Chapter Six

Shortly before my date with Eileen, I reached out to Richie and told him I would need him for an airport job first thing in the morning. Too excited from my evening and the possibilities that existed, I nearly forgot to pack. The last time I left Wichita for any extensive length of time, I took one change of shirt, pants, socks, and underwear knowing that Uncle Sam would supply me with garments and just about everything else I would need. At that time, I was gone for a little over three years. The idea of a three- or four-day excursion had me confused and uncertain. Meeting a dubious photographer did not require the same wardrobe as making a professional impression in front of another city's police officers. There were likely hacks all around that city, even more so than Wichita. In contemplating a city over ten times the size of my own hometown, I started to slowly feel lost, and I hadn't even left my apartment.

The cats, Lady Mittens and Sir Pounce, had looks on their face of disappointment as though they somehow knew I would be leaving them for a bit. I could not figure out how they knew unless they were imbued with powers of perception by the Almighty. Nothing in the Talmud could verify that. Then again, I learned never to doubt the powers of a cat.

I woke up early, a routine from my army days. I made coffee and a couple of scrambled eggs, and filled the cats' bowls with water and food. As I stepped out of the building's front door, I didn't find Richie waiting patiently and dutifully as expected. What stood out was an almost brand-new coupe with a suave-looking carefree gentleman in good spirits as he exited the vehicle. He strode up the walkway with an air of confidence. He had the physique of a heavyweight boxer who had retired several years prior and had gained a paunch from living high on the hog. He had dark, slicked-back hair, likely done with a popular treatment such as Wildroot Cream Oil. His black moustache appeared perfectly trimmed à la John Gilbert. This man made it known he knew more than me without uttering a single word. In my mind, I still needed proof.

"I let your boy know you wouldn't be needing him," he said as he stuck out his hand. He had yet to introduce himself despite admitting he altered my plans without asking me. It came across as either assurance or arrogance. Both bothered me.

"And why is that?"

"Waste of your time heading to LA." I looked at him perplexed. I made my decision to travel to the West Coast only recently and known only to, at most, three people. "I'm Max Burke." He grabbed my hand and shook it as though he tried to wring a towel dry. "I'm a private dick, just like you." That comment did not impress me.

"If it's all the same to you, Mr. Burke…"

"Look, it'll take you a day and a half, at the very least, to get out there." I looked at him perplexed. "You didn't check the schedules, did you?" My confusion did not clear up. "Braniff doesn't go there direct and neither does Continental. You'll have to fly to Denver or

Albuquerque and then connect with someone else. If you can find someone else. And if you miss that connection, you'll be hanging around Duke City or the Mile High City for an extra day, taking in the sights and adding to your expense account. Assuming your clients can afford it."

Truth be told, I hadn't checked the schedules and went into this rather blindly, a grievous error. I didn't admit it to him, however.

"Is there some place we can grab a belt?" he said rather drolly.

"It's seven thirty a.m. On a Sunday morning."

"What, you gotta go to church or something?"

"I'm Jewish."

"Like I said."

At this point, I had no ride to the airport other than this man's car. I obviously was unaware of flight schedules. I soon realized I would be out of my element even with the limited information I had about Debra Rose Nathan's activities in California. I hated the thought of not following through on what I considered a logical next step. But whatever this brash man knew might be useful enough to assist in my efforts, considering he already showed me what he knew. I needed to figure out his intentions. That could only be done if I accompanied him someplace where we could talk.

We got in his car, and I directed him to the King's X down on First and Broadway. I started toward the counter when I saw Jennie Palmer, but Mr. Burke grabbed my arm and guided me toward a booth in the far corner. He sat with his back to the wall. He hadn't reminded me of Wild Bill Hickok in either appearance or attitude, but he shared some of the same characteristics. I did not see Jack McCall anywhere in sight.

Burke was blustery when Jennie came out to take our order. She wasn't nearly as fazed by him as I had been.

"Two eggs, sunny up. Four slices of toast, heavy butter. A pile of home fries. And two orders of bacon." He turned to me. "I don't suppose you'll be having any?" He turned back to Jennie. "And coffee. Black coffee. And keep it coming, sweetie." Jennie took the menus and walked away. Burke said, "She didn't take your order."

"You're a private dick?" I commented.

He wagged his finger at me like I was a naughty child.

"You're a regular," he responded. "Should have figured being in the neighborhood and all. All right. We'll chalk up one for you."

"Mr. Burke…"

"Max."

"Max, you've sent away my transportation to the airport. You've tried to convince me it would be a waste of my time flying to Los Angeles on what is assuredly my private business. And you haven't told me anything to make me want to sit here and watch you gorge yourself on a ridiculous amount of food that only Abe Coleman, the Hebrew Hercules, would eat. Please make every effort to convince me. Otherwise I'll be on my way before you have your heart attack."

He put his hands on the table, perhaps to identify a willingness to parlay, and stared at me straight. The persona changed to moderately professional and somewhat confessional.

"I'm looking for Debra Rose Nathan." He said nothing further and simply patiently waited for my reaction or response. My face went slack and I nodded in understanding. He took that as a cue to continue. "You'd be wasting your client's money by taking a trip that won't tell you any more than I can."

"Who are you working for?"

He smiled and took his hands off the table.

"That is one thing I can't tell you. Of course, you of all people understand that."

He did everything possible to place us on equal ground despite the vast differences in our personalities and modes of operation.

My plate with two hard boiled eggs and my bowl of oatmeal with a sliced banana and strawberries looked like an anthill beside the mountain of food that took up rent in front of Max Burke. I had to admit he had manners for all the loud and gregarious behavior previously exhibited. We ate in silence as Jennie returned to fill Max's coffee cup six times. He let out a satisfied sigh, wiped his lips gingerly with his napkin, dipped his fingers in his water glass, and then tossed the napkin on the empty plate. After Jennie cleared the table, Max began his recitation to bring me up to speed.

"You know how many girls come out to California every year, every month, every week, all looking to break into the movies? Downright crazy. And most of them, I can tell you, do not have a pinky's worth of talent. Some of them don't even look any good for that matter. But what they all got is a body. I guarantee you there is one photographer for every fifty girls that get off a Greyhound bus with tinsel in their eyes."

"Girlie mags?"

"Girlie mags. Skin mags. Stag mags. You got names like *Beauty Parade*, *Titter*, *Flirt*, *Wink*, *Eyeful*, *Whisper*. The girls think the more they show, the better their chances are some legit producers admire their, shall we say, talents. These photos just wind up in cheap mags and the girls, well, some make good money and even stay in the business. The rest go home crying to their mommas."

"And that's what happened to Debra Rose Nathan?"

"Well, that has been the thought floating around in my head."

Definitely the wrong response. Max Burke could see I sensed it. If it was so difficult to fly from the Wichita to the West Coast, or vice versa, why would he have gone through all that difficulty on an assumption? Too much of an effort for an uncertainty. While I respected the privacy afforded to a client by a private detective, I had thus far not been aware of anyone else in Debra Rose's family or circle of friends who would warrant someone like a Max Burke in her life.

"I did some work with one of those photographers," he continued, smoothly but with a bit of a hiccup. "Guy named Brooks Mellon."

Donald Long referenced the same name. This turned out to be the first real connection to Debra Rose, and I certainly didn't let on I knew.

"What kind of work?"

"Divorce stuff. I found the cheating husband, or wife, and he got the photos."

I harbored no contempt. I did similar work in the beginning after I returned from the war. Perhaps my style was less cheap and gaudy.

"I kind of figured what he might have been up to,

but as long as it didn't involve me, I didn't say anything. Well, good old Brooks Mellon got himself murdered. And about that time, Miss Nathan left Los Angeles. On top of that, some film is missing from Mellon's studio. You see where I'm going with this?"

You did not need to be a private detective to follow his train of thought. The problem I had was the limited information forced me into only one direction. I knew from experience many roads led to either shamayim or sheol. I could not let this man pigeonhole my train of thought.

"Isn't this a police matter, Mr. Burke?"

"Well, yeah, for the most part you could say so."

"I did just say so."

He gave me an unappreciative smirk.

"Except my client is more interested in recovering the film than in getting involved in a homicide investigation. That is where I come in. You see, we're all for letting justice be done if other interests are served, shall we say."

He enunciated as smoothly as a Roman orator who spoke in jazz lingo.

"If the film is of Miss Nathan, doesn't she have a right to it?"

He leaned back with a smug self-satisfied grin on his face.

"I don't know about you, Mr. Bergman, but I'm no lawyer. My only job is to recover the film. Now, you're looking for Debra Rose and I'm looking for the film. Seems to me like we have a mutual interest."

"Not necessarily," I said while I stood up. He had a look on his face as though his dirigible had just been punctured.

"What do you mean?" he blathered.

"I mean I don't know enough about you, your client, or your interest in this. Until then, I'm safer on my own. And so, too, I presume, will Debra Rose be."

"We'll see."

He stood up, pulled a sizeable bankroll out of his pocket, peeled off a couple of bills, and threw them on the table. He stormed out as though I had called his mother an insulting name. Jennie came up behind me after the exchange.

"He's been here over a week," she said mildly. "Last Saturday, the fifteenth, he came in for breakfast. Had the same thing." This was a surprising revelation as I had only met Don Long and Arlene Nathan on the eighteenth, this past Tuesday.

I had half a mind to figure out a way to go to Los Angeles and check out this Brooks Mellon murder. That would be an incredible expense of time and money to get straight facts that I could acquire over the phone or through a telegram. For that, I could ask Clarence Mendenhall to reach out to his contacts and get me some dope on the case. That would be just as good. He might be able to look up this Max Burke as well. Then again, Carla Duggan could use phone directories from around the country to make an assessment on whether he was legit or not. In both cases, these inquiries would have to be deferred as Mendenhall didn't work Sunday afternoons and the library was not open. Max Burke would have to remain a mystery for at least another day.

I walked back the few blocks to my apartment. I couldn't say the cats were happy to see me, but they were pleasantly surprised. I took a bit to unpack my suitcase. I had to wonder who would hire a private detective to recover what likely were stag photos of Debra Rose Nathan. It really made no sense unless someone tried to hold that over on the girl for some unknown reason. Was she guilty of murder? Was that why she came back in a frenzy to Wichita and hardly said anything to her mother? I didn't want to believe it, but I couldn't be certain. Every possibility might lead to the truth. Not every question had an answer.

The only thing I knew for certain was that Max Burke hadn't told me everything. I realized I let my emotions get the better of me and hadn't played that scene out too well. I lost an opportunity to perhaps string him along. At the very least I could have learned where he was staying. Since he knew where I lived, I'd have to look over my shoulder for a big man with an even bigger attitude.

Chapter Seven

I high-tailed it down to police headquarters early on Monday and tried to get hold of Mendenhall before he knocked off from his shift. A night of plowing through the worst the city had to offer would run anyone ragged. And to think Clarence wanted me to join his squad. I had to bypass any sustenance, either at home or King's X. The cats, on the other hand, were well fed. That seemed to be my mandate.

Mendenhall looked more tired than usual. His position on the newly formed Night Detective Squad usually uplifted him. He told me once how exhilarating it was to be awake when all decent men and women were sleeping comfortably in their homes while he and his crew were out cleaning up the city streets. I wondered if he thought that way or if they were the rehearsed lines a public relations firm hired by the city came up with.

Strangely, I had that feeling at one time. Twenty-five years old and inching my way toward my dream job of detective inspector in the Wichita Police Department. Sure, I might have been relatively young, but I impressed enough people to give myself a chance to make it within a year or two. Then, Pearl Harbor changed my whole perspective. I couldn't rightly tell if I wished to be where he was.

"Hey, Mendenhall, can you do me a favor?"

He tipped his hat back off his forehead and looked

at me wearily. At this point, it wasn't about being tired.

"Maybe."

"You got any friends out in LA?"

"I might. Why?"

"Well, I can either take a day and a half and waste my client's money on maybe having a door closed in my face, or…"

"Or I can make a phone call and sweet-talk them."

I smiled and nodded.

"What is it?"

I laid out the story of Brooks Mellon and his murder, mentioned Max Burke, and conveniently left out Debra Rose Nathan. In describing the nature of Mellon's work, I figured Clarence assumed the nature of my case. Being a solid professional and a friend, he did not inquire further.

"What?" he asked when I just stood there in anticipation.

"Aren't you gonna call them?"

He looked at his wrist-watch. "It's five thirty out there. In the morning."

"So, their homicide department is closed for the night?"

"My acquaintance is not what you would call an early bird. I'll leave a report with the desk sergeant for you. You can pick it up around noon."

They say patience is a virtue. I tried hard to be virtuous. It was an ongoing process.

My patience started to wear thin as it approached eight a.m. The Wichita Carnegie Library would be open soon. It could be just as likely Carla Duggan would not be there so promptly. That inspired me to visit Rabbi Saperstein. He did not run by the hands of the clock.

The Rebbe was the most austere thing in the simple building of the Hebrew Congregation of Wichita. To call him "venerable" would be an understatement. I honestly did not know his age. He might have already passed Methuselah. He would always greet me by taking my hands in the act of blessing me. Whether I came to him as a policeman, a soldier, or a private detective, it was his honor to bless me. I learned so much from him and knew there was much more to learn. I could partake of such teachings by regular attendance at the temple. I needed to learn how not to be so stubborn.

He stood near the bimah and turned when he heard the synagogue doors open. I started to walk toward him briskly but found myself surprised when he did not immediately recognize me. Only when I was perhaps five feet from him did a smile appeared on his face and his outstretched hands welcomed me.

"Harold, your presence always gives me great delight. Come, sit."

Holding me by one hand, the elderly father of the temple guided me toward a seat in the front. Our voices, in normal tones, echoed in the emptiness. It sounded both solemn and majestic.

"So, *nu*, what in your heart brings you here today?"

"Simply to see my rabbi."

"Your respect and courtesy are well known. But you could see me more regularly at Shabbos services." I smiled. He did not seem to acknowledge the smile. His gaze fell more over my shoulder than directly at me. I moved slightly to one side and then the other to see if I got a response. "And by now," he continued austerely, "you have surmised there is an issue. But rather than coming out with a direct question, you move about like a gadfly. In the Talmud it is written *He who has the least understanding has the most questions*."

At this moment, I knew no greater truth than that.

"Your sight, Rabbi?" I asked in hushed tones.

"It is starting to fail me." I hung my head. He could see that gesture. With his hands beneath my chin, he lifted my head up. "There is a Jewish proverb which states: Growing old, man's sight worsens, but this allows him to see more."

"How?" I asked bluntly with the impetuousness of youth.

"Think back to your time as a soldier. You may not have seen the enemy clearly, identified him among the trees or behind rocks, but his presence was there. The Lord guided your aim. Consider what you do now as a detective. You seek the truth which is not always so easy to see, especially when so many work to hide it from us. We put too much faith in what our senses offer and less on what is in our hearts. The Lord guides us in all things, Harold."

Such notions were easier for an elderly man of faith to say. What I had encountered in Europe, what made it so difficult for me to just simply return to the police force and held me back from rabbinical college was the fact that my senses allowed me to see the uncertainty of things, an imbalance that seemed contrary to the will of the Lord. I still sought some clarity in this world, a stronger calling that would resonate deep within me. Until now, I had always thought it would take my senses to achieve that. Now, I wasn't sure.

We sat and spoke for a bit. He asked me about my father, inquired if I spent enough time with him, and, without requiring the details, asked how my current profession held up. I provided him the same reassurance that I would for any elder who I respected and admired. I left him with but a morsel of encouragement and a hope to find greater understanding.

It suddenly occurred to me I had a terrific hunger. It wasn't quite noon, so I had a good chance of getting a table at King's X and beat the lunch crowd. Jennie Palmer fixed me up with a grilled cheese sandwich and an iced tea. I sat in a booth by a window, the same booth where I had an unappealing breakfast with Max Burke. I almost gagged on my sandwich while that recollection swirled around in my mind. I needed to return my focus to that conversation, not the menu.

A grubby man in a cheap overcoat shuffled in and stood alongside my table. Taking him for a vagrant, I disregarded him for a bit. A scratchy throat sound like someone who gargled with rusty razor blades drew my attention.

"Long time no see, huh?"

I looked up at him and barely made out the features of Mickey Dowell. A good fifteen years older than me or more, he had been a sergeant in the police department until an ethics violation lost him his job and certification to be in law enforcement anywhere in the state of Kansas. He wasn't a bad sort that I knew of, not a drinker or foul-mouthed instigator. Whatever he had done, however, revealed a streak of moral turpitude, the likes of which made him unfit for duty. This was in the judgement of those who made such decisions. I had no say in the matter and did not care to have one now. Unfortunately, he stood stock still, unwilling to move.

"Hello, Mickey. What have you been up to?"

He took the brief polite inquiry as an invitation and

sat down opposite me. I gestured over to Jennie for a cup of coffee. He looked like he needed a lot more.

"Knocking around, here and there. Can't get a dick's license like you, but I make out okay." The icicle went from winter to summer in a moment. He simply melted. He nodded politely as Jennie set the coffee down, then quickly walked away. "As a matter of fact, there's a fella wants me to help find a girl for him."

"Good for you. I'm sure you'll do just fine."

The encouragement did not get my point across.

"Says you got a handle on this and won't play ball with him."

Realizing this character tried to make a cheap dollar from Max Burke by facing up to me was annoying. I leaned forward and glared at him. It wasn't my style to play Mike Mazurki with anyone, but I thought Mickey would fall for it.

"If you're talking about a cold fish named Burke, he's a knucklehead who doesn't know bupkis. He walks around like a butter and egg man, but he's nothing more than a bindle stiff." From the sound of it, I was ready to go to Hollywood and star in the pictures. Move aside, Jimmy Cagney!

"So, you're saying you don't know nothin'."

"I'm saying there is nothing to tell." He gulped down the java and stood up to leave. I grabbed his arm as much out of sympathy as concern. "Mickey, you watch out for this guy. He's from LA and I don't think he's playing you straight."

He pulled his arm away, straightened his overcoat, and walked out. I looked over at Jennie who was decidedly happy by his departure.

It was just yesterday when this Max Burke upended

my plans to go to California to learn about Debra Rose Nathan's activities there. Burke freely advised about a photographer's murder, insinuated Debra Rose could be involved, and swore he looked for some film and nothing more. By not flying out there, I had to take his word, temporarily at least. I still had half a mind to make that trip after all. If I decided to do so, tomorrow was my birthday, after all. It might make a nice present to myself.

Carla Duggan moved around faster than a pollinating bee in an English garden. She held several volumes in her arms, deposited some upon the desks of various patrons, picked up others, and stopped to chatter and, naturally, pass on sage advice. Ever since I had known her, she had a passion for knowledge and information. There would be no better place for her to work. Unless the government needed espionage agents.

When she saw me, she gasped. She put her pile of books down on some patron's desk, scurried to me quickly, grabbed me by the arm, and whisked me to her tiny, cramped office no bigger than a broom closet. She sat down and crossed her arms defiantly.

"What have you gotten me into?"

"Would you be so kind as to clarify that comment?"

"Sharon and Martin Kaye."

"What? Are they Bonnie and Clyde?"

"Not quite. But just about."

Her response to my facetiousness caught me off guard. She pushed over a rather uncomfortable wooden chair, and I sat beside her as she pulled out a stack of newspapers. She showed me articles about financial misdeeds, suicides, public civics committees, and one court order from San Antonio, Shreveport, and Jacksonville. Then, she showed me other articles: from

Greensboro, North Carolina, a local judge filed a complaint against Susan and Mark King for fraud; from Charlottesville, Virginia, an obituary of an elderly seamstress whose relatives claimed a Sophia and Marcus Klingman had bilked her; and from Wilkes-Barre, Pennsylvania, a warrant issued for the arrest of Samantha and Michael Kronauer.

"You want me to dig further?" Carla now appeared gleeful at the results of her research. It was a thread that wound up taking apart an entire fabric. If the other three articles were indeed Sharon and Martin Kaye, it was heavy evidence that Mrs. Kaye hired me under false pretenses. They appeared, on the surface, to be criminally negligent individuals who engineered a long series of swindles involving investments, on the surface quite legitimate, but complex enough to confuse those with limited knowledge of such things. On the other hand, with such a background, it would be possible Mr. Kaye might have been the victim after he destroyed so many people's lives.

The question was whether Sharon Kaye would admit to their insidious past to help me locate her husband's killer. The thought then occurred to me she might be a likely target as well, threatened with death if she didn't make good on reimbursement or more.

Chapter Eight

I figured it might be too early to check in on whatever report Mendenhall gave to the desk sergeant, so I opted to visit Sharon Kaye. After my interviews with a couple of their clients and a consult with Carla Duggan, I figured there were a couple of approaches to take. I could be coy. That always popped up as the first thought and sometimes more preferred. It would not work, however, when you had a sly subject who knew more than you. You wound up as a piece of yarn being toyed with by a cat. I had intimate knowledge of that concept.

I could always come across as the intuitive professor with the Socratic method. Ask her questions, get responses, and then ask further leading questions from those responses. Then again, I couldn't come up with enough questions to ask when I wasn't adept enough on the nature of their financial business. The scene that played out in my mind: me all tongue tied after two questions and on the end of a questioning and disappointed look.

The direct approach, just throwing it out there and watch the reaction, could ultimately make me appear as mean and uncaring. An impassioned apology could take care of that, and it would avoid an unnecessary waste of time.

She greeted me graciously at the door to her apartment and welcomed me in. She did not offer anything, coffee or water, but directed me to the couch opposite the chair she sat in. She presented a completely professional front that also came across as rather aloof. At this point, I was her employee, and she treated me accordingly.

"Samantha and Michael Kronauer," I started. "Sophia and Marcus Klingman. Susan and Mark King."

She sat there with a blank look on her face. One eyebrow raised. Her head cocked to one side followed by a light shaking in abject confusion. The appearance of uncertainty might mask complete control. I tried hard not to be so cynical.

"Who are these people?"

"Greensboro. Charlottesville. Wilkes-Barre."

She shrugged her shoulders.

"These couples were implicated in confidence schemes over the past several years. They share yours and your late husband's initials. Additionally, they form a direct geographic path with Jacksonville, Shreveport, and San Antonio where you and Mr. Kaye admittedly were previously. And finally, here in Wichita."

"Similarity of names and geography are what you have to claim we are perpetrators as opposed to victims?" A shocked, almost breathless aspect exuded from her comment, the incredulity oozing out through her pores. It was either a woman hurt by an awful accusation or this year's Academy Award winning performance, Jennifer Jones in *Duel in the Sun* notwithstanding.

"I do not make assumptions, Mrs. Kaye. I dig up facts and present them in a logical order. From there, the truth eventually emerges." I sounded an awful lot like Rabbi Saperstein. Perhaps facing the possibility of a deceitful person got under my skin.

"And what is the truth as you see it, Mr. Bergman?"

"The coincidences are rather strong and were worth discussing. You and your husband never lived in Greensboro…?"

"Charlottesville or Wilkes-Barre, no."

"Where did you live before Jacksonville?"

She got up, paced, went to the coffee table, lit a cigarette, and then sat back down. I swore I recalled Mary Astor acting quite similarly in *The Maltese Falcon* with Sharon Kaye just as deliberate.

"If you have any doubts about my integrity, I'll gladly pay your fee and dismiss you."

If you waited long enough, someone always threw down the gauntlet. When you played poker, it was a bluff. In a battle, one of wits or physical strength, you came to the crossroads, that point in time when you had to decide: pursue or retreat. I had to determine this woman's real character and intentions. If they were as stated, I could continue on my path, and put aside the information Carla had retrieved for me. I was very conscious of a quote from the Talmud: *Don't do favors for evildoers, and no evil will befall you.* It was likely the word "knowingly" should be included, especially when I considered Albert Whitman.

"No, I don't, Mrs. Kaye. I hope you understand investigations of this sort can result in many unpleasant revelations. I had to determine what you knew in these matters. Without that, there are only assumptions. As I said, I deal in facts."

"I understand." She ground out her cigarette in the ashtray, arose, and held out her hand. She thanked me for stopping by, pleased I didn't rattle her cage too much, but sending me back out to search for a possible disgruntled client who took her husband's life. The clear signal it was time for me to leave.

I stood outside the Commodore, arms folded across my chest, and looked up, not that she would be able to see me. Since the police had pretty much written this case off as a suicide or perhaps accidental death, my only recourse would be to consider who stood to benefit. Cui bono. If it were, the question was why Martin Kaye would kill himself. Despondency or depression came to mind. So did financial loss. However, Sharon Kaye had never indicated any business irregularities or problems. The furnished apartment was far more costly than my own simple flat, and her wardrobe kept well within the standards of high society.

For the same reason, a homicide would either be one of passion, emotional distress, or the result of someone coming out ahead. Sure, an angry rube who considered himself cheated might fly off the handle and kill Kaye if there could be no chance of getting their money back or proving larceny. Perhaps a hired killer murdered him at the behest of Sharon Kaye so she could inherit…what? Insurance money? They did not own a home or have any lasting roots in any one community. I wasn't aware of any dalliance in her life through casual perusal of her place, no tell-tale evidence of a peccadillo. Even so, her husband's passing with what amounted to the police's blessing would leave her free to carry on. Why then would she hire me?

Everything I could think of circled back around to nothing that made sense. Any experienced private detective would have cashed in the chips on this game and walked away from the table. My unyielding need to know the truth kept me moving forward. It might be in pieces of evidence or locked away deeply in Sharon Kaye's heart.

I walked casually back to police headquarters, figuratively scratching my head. As I crossed Douglas, I felt a twinge in my ankle. It was a beautiful day, and I walked at a relaxed pace. It seemed my emotional uncertainty translated itself into a more tangible feeling.

Melvin Bronsky, the desk sergeant, advised me that Mendenhall had gone home for the day after the initial calls to Los Angeles. At first, I was disappointed until Bronsky indicated a file awaited me.

I read Mendenhall's reasonably legible handwriting. According to the LAPD, Brooks Mellon died from internal injuries after a rather bad beating. With no weapon other than the assailant's fists and perhaps some brass knuckles, they had no worthwhile physical evidence like a bullet slug or sharp object. The photography studio was thoroughly ransacked; the perpetrator looked for something specific. At first, police assumed robbery as a motive but found nothing of any calculable value taken. Several expensive cameras were still there, a small amount of cash, and a jewelry box that contained extravagant necklaces apparently used in the photo shoots.

The police attempted to contact Mellon's partner, Maximillian Price Burke. I read the name repeatedly and knew I would have to consult with Mendenhall. These notes described Burke as Mellon's partner, which I had to assume meant in the photography business. Burke described himself as an investigator, like myself, working the seedier aspects of the photography business. I knew I couldn't trust him. Since I had brushed him off due to his uncouth manner, I had to wait for him to catch up with me again, which I was sure he would.

Unless I located Mickey Dowell and shook him down a bit. Burke indicated his search was only for stag photos on film. If he had hidden his real profession and misled me on other things, like a trip to California, I couldn't be sure what else he had lied about. If that truly happened, Debra Rose Nathan was not to blame. I guessed she took something else of value and these ne'er-do-wells ran a scam to keep it all quiet. That made the young lady an unwitting bit of interference. Her fate was undetermined at this point but considerably closer to jeopardy.

There were a couple of pool rooms I visited along with a few businesses, jewelry stores and knick-knack parlors, as well as about three pawn shops. Mickey would do anything to pick up a buck anywhere he could since he was in no position to get a legitimate job. Just outside a dive Italian restaurant on St. Francis, south of Second Street, I literally ran into him.

"What gives, shamus?' he blurted out in a rather friendly manner.

"Max Burke. I want to see him."

"Ready to play ball, huh?"

I grabbed him by the lapels.

"That is my business, Mickey. I'm sure you get a finder's fee if you set up a meet."

"All right. Fine. I'll send him by your place tomorrow night. Seven."

I let go of his clothing.

"Night after tomorrow," I uttered.

"What's wrong with tomorrow?"

"It's my birthday."

I walked in the direction of Douglas hoping to grab a cab. My foot really throbbed now. As I walked away, Mickey called back, "Hey, happy birthday!"

Chapter Nine

I had half a mind to get some work done. Anything I could consider would wind up as the distractions of well-wishers rather than significant conversation. That would have made any investigation effort useless.

So, on my thirtieth birthday, Tuesday, June 25, 1946, I largely stayed home until it was time to go over to my father's house for dinner. I fixed a couple of fried eggs over toast and a full pot of coffee. The cats were privy to some luscious cat food, and we all enjoyed our morning repast in relative peace. Their very presence was a gift enough for me.

Afterward, I tried to figure out what to read. I always kept the Old Testament nearby, but that kind of reflection did not strike my mood. Instead, I took out a small chapbook of *fin de siècle* poetry, seeking out the lyrical and beautiful. Unfortunately, I came face to face with the type of introspection not viable at such an early time of the day.

Ernest Dowson was both a noble and tragic figure. In one sense, almost pathetic. He had an unrequited obsession with a young uneducated restaurant worker. You couldn't even really call her a waitress. He seemed to write effortlessly but hardly made any effort to improve upon his lot in life. I came across one stanza which encapsulated his very being:

"They are not long, the days of wine and roses:

Out of a misty dream
Our path emerges for a while, then closes
Within a dream."

I began to wonder if it were more of a universal thought. So many comrades in arms perished, literally within the blinking of an eye. I could do nothing to prevent it, but neither had much time to reflect upon it. My life was at risk.

I used logic and intellect to figure things out at the behest of those who could afford to have me do so, those who had neither the time nor inclination, perhaps not even the passion necessary. Perhaps these cases were worthwhile on their own merit, significant in some way to the client. Then again, they might simply be subterfuge for a more heinous diversion, like the late Albert Whitman. The cases I undertook were other people's search for truth and meaning. While I tried to take them on as my own, I always realized my path would eventually lead elsewhere.

The poetry I had chosen to place me in a pastoral mood only served to make me look inward. Therefore, I reached out for my Bible to see what significance I could find on this, the day of my birth. My long-suffering friend Job showed me the way: *With the ancient is wisdom; and in length of days understanding.* Apparently, all I had to do was wake up each morning, get through my day, and eventually I would figure the whole thing out. Seemed simple enough.

All the while, Lady Mittens lay curled up beside me while the demonstrative Sir Pounce sat squarely in my lap after circling about several times. In those moments, I found complete peace. I met a woman whose husband died in possibly undetermined circumstances. I learned of a missing young girl who may have been in a bit of trouble. I had a fiduciary responsibility to ascertain the truth. Often, it was necessary to distance yourself from the sentence to read the entire story.

They say that scent is the thing that triggers memory the most. On this particular evening, I found that to be true. My mother's favorite dish to make was a white fish, usually halibut, dotted with pieces of butter, chopped parsley, and slivered almonds. The earthiness of it, she said, connected us after a fashion to the garden. Not the one we gave up after the temptation, but to the plants that gave us life. My father noticed my nose taking in the aroma. He gently laid his hand upon my arm.

"Your mother would have been proud of you." It was a touching thing to say, one that made me appreciate the blessings of my life.

On the table my father had a homemade challah, a small green salad in a bowl, and the plate with the fish and a rice pilaf. Surprisingly, there were two glasses of wine as well. I guess my birthday called for a celebration. My father recited prayers for the wine and the food, and I responded to each.

"*Barukh atah Adonai Eloheinu, Melekh ha'olam, bo're p'ri hagefen.*"

"Blessed are you, Lord our God, King of the universe, Who creates the fruit of the vine."

"*Barukh atah Adonai Eloheinu, Melekh ha'olam, sheakol nih'ye hidvaro.*"

"Blessed are you, Lord our God, King of the universe, through Whose word everything comes into being."

"Amen."

"Amen."

We ate mostly in silence except for a few sounds of satisfaction from both of us. I had an immediate memory of my last dinner at home after I enlisted. While I couldn't recall the exact meal, I had a distinct recollection of my mother doing everything she could to hold back her deep abiding concern for my well-being. She knew in her heart I did the right thing but could not help but feel she might never see me again. How could we know that would come to pass.

I helped my father clear the table and do the dishes despite his insistence I needn't do such things on my birthday. I commented on his delightful challah, but he gave me a familiar look, the one that indicated it was nothing more than a simple act of baking.

We sat down in the parlor. He lit his pipe, a faint smile on his face. I could only smile in return.

"Are you happy, Harold?"

It was a question any parent would ask of their child. On this occasion, I surmised it might have more meaning behind it. As I sat there, I realized it wasn't an easy question to answer. I had a place to live, gainful employment, and a smattering of trust and respect I had earned by my deeds. What qualified as happiness?

"I'm working on that." I squinted in thought, then continued, "What I have learned, so far, is that there is little I can possess that provides any degree of satisfaction. Were I to own a home, I would not be any happier."

"What about a wife?" he asked slyly.

"Perhaps. But"—I went on to avoid that conversation—"to aid those around me, to offer my caring and compassion, to assist in setting right a wrong, this makes me happy in a way I cannot possibly describe.

Tzedakah. To do what is right and just. That is about all I seem to think about right now."

"Your nobility is greater than your years." My pride swelled at his pronouncement. "But it is said that all of us will render an account before the Lord of all the good he beheld in life but chose not to enjoy." He leaned forward, almost in the same manner as Bradley Wolrebinski, but in a far sweeter manner. "You are young. You have been through much already. The world is safer because of men like you. When will you reap the rewards of your efforts?"

I heard my father encouraging me to grab life by the lapels, shake it up, and discover the beauty and richness of all creation. It was a very endearing notion. Yet, I found it hard to explain to him how being a policeman had shown me a side of life buried underneath a shroud to most folks; how the war brought to the light the darkest instincts that man is capable of. Once I had seen and experienced all of that, I could find no rewards. Only further questions. The real irony lay in the Bible filled with stories of wanderers. Cain and those who fled bondage in Egypt. Most of those were driven away by their sin. What was mine?

At the end of the evening, my father held my head in his hands and looked at me deeply. Perhaps he tried to see a part of himself or maybe see who I really was. I thanked him for the meal, which he shrugged off once again. He made no further mention of attending Sabbath services or bringing up inquiries as to Eileen's welfare. He trusted I would come about when the dust had settled on my uncertainties.

Here before me stood the man who brought me into the world thirty years prior. For that entire time, he gave me the benefit of knowledge, a deep abiding sense of responsibility to those around me, and an appreciative heart. Such a legacy I would always treasure.

I walked up to Douglas and hailed a cab. I had a small notion to stop by the Pan-American, but I couldn't possibly eat any of the rich dessert King Mar would have unloaded on me. I simply went home to the loving ministrations of my beloved felines. I took off my shoes and sat down for a bit, allowing them to peruse and play.

The celebratory night ended. I turned thirty years of age. Tomorrow, there was more to do.

Chapter Ten

The next morning, I was thirty years and a day. I brushed my teeth, combed my hair, and looked in the mirror. I found no perceptible change.

I figured to go back to the spot by the river where they found Martin Kaye. There were too many uncertainties about that case, too many possibilities in either direction to create doubt as to whether I would be able to completely prove his manner of death. I could not discern any viable evidence to put me in a proper direction. After a quick breakfast of toast and coffee, I rubbed the cats' ears and headed off to the Pan American to retrieve my car.

Midweek found the park almost empty, making it easy for me to stop off at a brief distance and meander around without anyone posing inquiries. I crouched down, stared in the direction of my bent knees, looked back over my shoulder, lifted my head high to see the curb from the embankment, and generally acted as though afflicted with Saint Vitus' Dance. I needed imagine Martin Kaye, what he might have experienced, and how he would have responded, drunk or sober.

A sudden turn on my heels, and I caught the eye of a man who stood at the curb about twenty feet from me. His brown suit fit poorly and could have used a sponge. The loosened tie around the collar would be the relaxed appearance of a man at the end of the day, only it was the middle of the morning. The hat pushed up on his forehead revealed a layer of sweat not typical for ten a.m. Even from this distance, I saw eyes glazed over and reddish. His hands in his pockets, he rocked on his heels and smiled at me.

"Funny how you can look at something from all angles and still don't see anything different."

"Yeah. Funny," I responded. "I don't suppose you'd mind telling me who you are."

He started toward me, slowly and uncertainly, shifting on his feet as he moved. If I didn't know better, I could have sworn he was intoxicated. When he moved closer and extended his hand, I realized the truth from his breath.

"My apologies. Kelly Gardner. Farmers and Bankers Life Insurance."

"I don't need any," I said after shaking his sweaty hand.

"What? Oh." He laughed. I never thought of myself as that humorous. Maybe it takes a certain type of audience. "No. I'm the adjuster for the Martin Kaye policy."

I could not imagine this man employed in any position by an insurance company or for any respectable firm given his appearance and intoxicated state. Until I could figure out his play, I led him in the direction of telling his own story.

"What does an adjuster do?" I asked, not all that concerned with the answer. In the middle of my own inquiry, I didn't have too much time for someone else unless he planned to get in the way or help me out.

"Well, the police are calling it suicide, and Mrs. Kaye thinks he was murdered, and I'm trying to figure it all out."

"How about that? So am I."

He looked at me as though he tried to break a code. Perhaps he thought he knew me or tried to discern my motives as well.

"You're the private investigator she hired?"

"Yes." Brevity was the key to ending this drab conversation. Or so I thought.

"She wants you to prove murder."

"Of course."

"Well, I'm inclined to agree with you."

That caught me off guard. One would typically think the insurance companies would do everything in their power to save a buck. In this case, accept the police report of suicide to avoid paying out on a life insurance policy. Perhaps in his inebriated state, Mr. Gardner revealed more than he should have. Not knowing him, I could not figure out any other reason for his complete openness.

"What is your take on it?" I asked, having almost come to a dead end in my own investigation and happy to let him go on like a ticker tape if he so desired.

"I have a report of a rather heated discussion between Mr. Kaye and an unidentified individual in Mr. Kaye's office on the afternoon of his death. While we have no exact information on who it might be or the specifics of the conversation, it appeared to be very threatening in nature."

"Where did this report come from?"

He smiled and gave it his best effort to look coy. He mostly came across as tired.

"Regrettably, I am not at liberty to divulge that information."

"Well, what physical evidence do you have to counter the official police report?"

"Unfortunately…" I held up my hand to stop him before he became a parrot.

"If you're so sure Mr. Kaye was murdered, there is really no reason for me to continue taking Mrs. Kaye's money if the claim is going to be settled."

For a moment, Gardner's demeanor went from slack to upright, tired to impassioned.

"My investigation relates solely to the claim. Don't you think, beyond that, Mrs. Kaye would want justice to be served?"

He was dead serious, and he had a point. My work had nothing to do with the insurance aspect of it. However, if she were right and her husband had been murdered, I would be remiss if I didn't do everything I could to find his killer or, at the very least, seek out enough evidence to bring to the police. From Kelly Gardner, I acquired a renewed sense of responsibility in this matter.

I stood in the lobby of police headquarters on William Street. My head swiveled like a kitten chasing its tail. For a good portion of my young adult life, this was like a second home, my supervisors and a few older police officers as substitutes for the uncles I never had. The place where I had the most comfort, knowing that laws were created to provide order to our world. My experience in Europe made all that moot.

By spinning around, in my oblivion I bumped into Bill Ward of the Night Detective Squad. He caught me before I fell.

"And Mendenhall wants you back on the force?" he joked.

"Just getting back from night duty?"

He tipped his hat up off his forehead, looking worn out from what must have been a rough night. I knew better than to ask simply out of idle curiosity. If a detective wanted to talk, he would just to relieve himself of a burden. If he did not, it was because he wanted to bury the day.

"Tracking down a bank robber. Do you believe those kinds of guys are still out there? I thought that kind of stuff ended with Dillinger."

I shrugged.

"You know anything about a Martin Kaye? You guys pegged it as suicide."

"Well, that is the official report based on the coroner's examination. And all because the wound on the head was not considered what they call a 'striking blow.' But I can't figure a guy, even a drunk guy, being so lucky as to fall directly on a stone and crack his skull open."

"Who would have killed him?"

"I couldn't tell you. But since that case is currently closed, we've got to move on to the next one." He patted me on the arm. "See you around, kid."

Adding in the encounter with Kelly Gardner, that was all I needed to pursue this investigation as far as it would take me. That didn't mean I had any more to go on. For now, I simply decided to take the drive out to El Dorado to interview another one of the Kaye's clients.

The experience wasn't as pleasant or laid back as Horatio Frazier or Reginald Kraft. This time, Arnold Sims practically impressed me as a possible suspect right off the bat. A short and bookish man, he wore a tight-fitting paisley vest over a starched white shirt and tie with a very tight Windsor knot. Perhaps he had cut off his circulation and the lack of oxygen to his brain made him act crazy. Maybe he was just plain crazy. His face wasn't red, and he didn't spit as he spoke. He acted more like a runaway train in terms of his attitude.

"Scoundrels. Nothing but scoundrels." He used the word as an invective. "I started with a thousand dollars. Seemed appropriate given the return on investment promised. Then they wanted another five hundred. I acquiesced once until they came back a week later and encouraged me to invest another five hundred. I was still within the thirty-day period to withdraw my funds. But by the time they returned my calls, that window had closed. I could not tell if that was intentional or simply an unfortunate occurrence. They assured me repeatedly, however, of the safety of my investment. Repeatedly, mind you." He gathered his breath before blurting out "Scoundrels" one final time.

"What do you do for a living, Mr. Sims?"

"I'm an accountant for Citizens Bank."

"Did you find anything about their prospectus that seemed suspect in any fashion, at least to your knowledge?"

"No, not to my knowledge. Then again, their form of investing was beyond the scope of my familiarity. They used actuarial terms and financial lingo that seemed entirely valid. Perhaps even designed to be that way. I had made a few inquiries from co-workers who had some small experience in these matters. The Vice President of the bank is a very good friend of mine and recommended I take another course of action. A more legal one. Although if it were up to me, I would replicate Carrie Nation's actions."

I couldn't see Arnold Sims wielding an axe and tearing up a business office, perhaps removing fingers from hands. Then again, I had been wrong before. By this one visitation, the groundwork was there for a reasonable possibility of an angry investor, one willing go to a greater extreme. It didn't have to be someone big and brutish, just pushed to their emotional limits, like Sims. Without full information on the actual biographies of the Kayes, I couldn't assume any other motive, nor could I eliminate an alternative altogether.

I went back to their office and rummaged through files looking for more investors. There were two approaches to take. Those individuals with more to lose might take more aggressive action. Then again, a small-time investor, offering his life savings, even if it were only a scant couple of hundred dollars, might feel desperate enough to act out and seek vengeance. I leaned toward the wealthier client perhaps due to my natural aversion to such folks. It wasn't too long ago I faced off against Albert Whitman, a man who willingly sacrificed his daughter for his own greed. I knew how those of prosperity could go to extremes to maintain their lifestyle.

There were two clients in College Hill, one in Riverside, an affluent farmer in Rose Hill, and the president of a refinery out in Augusta. I gathered these files before realizing it was late. I expected a visit from Max Burke at seven that evening. I would have just enough time to grab a bite to eat and head home.

I knew of a canteen in Union Station, practically across the street. I jaywalked on Douglas and grabbed a seat at the counter. A chicken salad sandwich and a cup of coffee would get me through the night. Either that or commiserating with Burke at a downtown eatery. I did not relish the notion of watching him gorge himself on a feast. I also needed to get back and feed the cats before that adventure began.

I drove the car back to the Pan American and walked back home, shlepping an armful of folders to research at my earliest possible convenience. After I attended to the felines' dinner, I put the files in my bedroom and then shut the cats up behind the pocket doors. I didn't want them subject to Burke's brusqueness. They deserved a better quality of guests.

I heard a car pull up abruptly to the sidewalk followed by the slam of a car door. It sounded like the overbearing tones of Mr. Burke. I stepped out of my apartment and opened the front door to the building. It was not who I expected.

Chapter Eleven

The man was almost as heavy-set as Burke but walked with a certain air about him, as though every step he took were on sacred ground, something difficult enough with his bulk. He wore a dark gray pin-striped suit, deep purple shirt with matching handkerchief, black tie, and black shoes. His hat had a pale white band around it. If I didn't know any better, I could have sworn he was a dandy, perhaps a Caucasian Zoot Suit boy. Maybe even a pimp. Instead, I recognized him as Ralph Dewald, local businessman, failed candidate for city council, and man of some importance at least in his own mind. He strode up to me as though I eagerly expected him. That wasn't the case.

"Mr. Bergman," he proclaimed loudly, sticking out his hand as though it were a bayonet. I shook it, sweat and all, as a courtesy. It took everything I had to keep from wiping it on my pants.

"Mr. Dewald, correct?" I used a softer tone to encourage him to reduce his volume. I looked over his shoulder as though I waited for the punchline.

"Am I catching you at a bad time?"

"I was expecting someone, and strangely enough, it didn't happen to be you."

"Well, if you will allow me a brief moment of your time, I will depart when your expected visitor appears." He didn't wait for a response nor an invitation, just simply walked past me and into my apartment. He had sat down by the time my surprise and annoyance wore off.

"What can I do for you?" I replied quietly yet politely.

"There seems to be a lot of misinformation flying around these parts with regard to a theft in California."

"Go on." I took this as a sign of a poor poker player. He practically told me the cards in his hand figuring I would just fold. I wasn't ready to admit to knowledge of anything, considering he just referenced misinformation. The people who play their cards close to the vest do not often lay them out on the table.

"I'm not going to insult your intelligence, Mr. Bergman. I imagine a scurrilous character named Max Burke has likely contacted you about an item of some sort stolen from the recently deceased Brooks Mellon in Los Angeles, a less than reputable photographer. I can only assume said item described as inconsequential."

"Stag photos of a young lady of good character from a good family can hardly be called inconsequential."

"In the scope of the larger picture, they are." He clearly stated his position, lacking emotion, but dismissive, nevertheless. That was the second thing that made me not like him.

I heard the cats' mew behind the pocket doors. I had a notion they recognized the tone of the visitor as one not appropriate to their domain. They likely would have used their claws to good purpose had they the chance. Fortunately for Mr. Dewald, he had me alone to deal with.

"I'm concerned with a mother and daughter in Kansas, the young lady's reputation and hopes for the future. So, what is the larger picture, Mr. Dewald?"

He took in a deep breath and exhaled it just as quickly, perhaps put off by having to explain the dynamics of industry to a peon. I made him do so just the same.

"The late Mr. Mellon had his hands in many cookie jars, so to speak. You are already aware of his photographic business, which encompassed legitimate as well as nefarious products, none of which are my current concern. However, he was a fence as well as a thief and a contact for the Los Angeles underworld."

"Okay, I get it. Brooks Mellon was not a nice guy. Larger picture, Mr. Dewald. I've got another appointment. Remember?" My indignation grew heavier, surpassing Dewald's heft and the humid air outside.

"Industrial espionage. The stolen photos contained plans for a new hydroelectric generator that would result in more efficient production. Whoever has those plans, as well as the means to build it, both logistically as well as financially, will secure a huge government contract easily worth several millions."

"All we got here is the Arkansas River. I don't see that keeping the lights on." Perhaps I allowed my voice to sound like a backwoods moonshiner from Oklahoma. This pompous recitation became more boring, a waste of my time, and took me away from a possible negotiation with Max Burke. On top of that, I couldn't see any connection to Debra Rose Nathan's disappearance other than the late Brooks Mellon.

"There are, shall we say, business interests here in Sedgwick County who have the means to create a plant to mass produce these generators. The war effort has provided us with a surplus of manufacturing capability as well as an abundance of workers. That won't last forever."

"Who owns these plans? I mean, who do they really belong to."

The politicians' façade started to melt. He reverted to a patent medicine salesman whose pitch fell apart with the truth.

"Do you understand what this means for this city, Mr. Bergman?"

"I'm getting the idea I understand what it means to you."

"I can't afford to let Max Burke get his hands on that film. He would sell it to the highest bidder. And that could mean anyone. I'm not willing to take that chance."

I looked aimlessly out the window.

"I'm expecting someone, Mr. Dewald."

With an exaggerated huff, he stood up, popped his hat on his head in an awkward angle, and walked out. I followed and watched him get into his car and drive away. I figured I hadn't seen the last of him.

As I started to close the front door, I heard a whispered "psst" from just off to the side of the building.

"Bergman."

Max Burke stepped out from the shadows. On this mildly warm night, he sweated too much for it to be just humidity. His eyes darted all over the place but never rested in my direction. Since we met, I had been foremost on his mind. Now I seemed secondary.

"How long have you been there?"

He came up the steps faster than the cats and rushed past me saying "Let's get inside."

He was no longer the blustery bigwig from the West

Coast with more bravado than brains. He turned into a worm on a hook about to get dipped in the river. He didn't seem pleased to be nibbled on by any bigger fish.

"Were you listening outside the window? Are you a peeper as well?"

"I saw a fancy car and an ace step out, so I knew I needed to find out his action."

"So, stag photos or business plans?" My hands on my hips akimbo, the cats' mews grew even louder. I had a good mind to just let them loose. It would likely have done very little good.

"To be honest, I don't know what they are."

My hands dropped to my side while an exaggerated gasp escaped my lips.

"You and Brooks Mellon were partners. Weren't you?"

"Yes."

"But you didn't know what he was involved with?"

"I had an idea. Look, he used me for what he needed. Sure, I snooped around the studio but with so much stuff, so many phone calls, so many visitors, I couldn't keep track of what he was into. That little chippy was there one day, looked like she was hiding something. I questioned her and she ran out. I noticed some film gone. It seemed reasonable it might have been important."

To refer to Debra Rose Nathan as promiscuous really annoyed me but I didn't have the time or inclination to set him to rights. That would have to wait until later.

"So, you just simply assumed it was her stag photos."

"Mellon would get these girls drunk. Sometimes he would offer them reefers. After that, these birds would do anything. How did I know he had secret business plans as well?"

There were a couple of ways of looking at this. Max Burke had the notion he was on the hunt for girlie photos that he could use for blackmail or resale. However, the income earned from that wouldn't have justified a plane trip from LA He could have just as easily ransacked the photography studio and taken all the film and dealt with it right there. Then again, I didn't see him as a mastermind involved in espionage, just a dupe scurrying for a bigger payout. Whatever he knew, or thought he knew, sent him on this merry goose chase. Ralph Dewald had more insight but more reluctance to dole out info. For all I knew, his story was just as far-fetched as the Easter bunny.

I needed to find Debra Rose Nathan. Whatever she had was hot and burning a hole in her hand. Pretty soon, the flame would consume her.

Max Burke exposed himself as a hustler but at the very least one more amenable to the idea I could work with him. For now, he would work this from his angle and me from mine. This time I determined he checked in at the Manhattan Hotel.

Just as with Dewald, I watched Burke exit the building and walk to the end of the block where he had parked after he saw the other car and my unannounced visitor. How unfortunate to consider a scared young lady had inadvertently become involved in a large scheme by men who had no compunction about eliminating her as a minor inconvenience. I saw that scary notion directly with Whitman and his daughter. I did not want to present the idea to Mrs. Nathan as it would likely send her over the edge. I needed to get a hold of Donald Long and update him on these latest happenings.

It wasn't practical to reach out to my contacts in the Wichita Police Department or directly with the Los Angeles Police Department either. Anything stolen would be crucial to a homicide investigation and certainly not shared with a civilian outsider from Kansas. Murder always trumped a missing persons case.

The vaguest notion occurred to me that my young runaway might be involved with Brooks Mellon's criminal activities. What if she showed greater comprehension and a willingness to assist him or through coercion to do so to prevent the release of the sensitive photos? Blackmail is a psychological tool used for more than just financial gain. Perhaps she was aware of or even a witness to Mellon's death and knew she needed to have an upper hand, anything with bargaining power.

Just as quickly, I dismissed the idea. I met her mother, talked with her, saw where they lived. I could easily imagine a bored teenager wanting to escape the drudgery of a life that seemed boxed in. I understood the stardust in her eyes that led her on a magic journey to a place where dreams came true, at least on the screen. I could picture the embarrassment of acquiescing to a plaintive yet unscrupulous request. I could not envision a maliciousness and deviant response. I had never met her but I had a strong impression of her.

At first, I couldn't accept the notion of Caroline Whitman and Dale Walker as pawns of a man so intent upon wealth and power that I saw them as victims only when it became too late. I didn't want Debra Rose Nathan to be an unwitting villain. Similarly, I didn't want her to be a victim either. All you can be in life is a villain, a victim, or a hero. Maybe she was the latter.

Bradley clearly outlined the two times Debra Rose ran off. These considerations of Brooks Mellon, Burke, and Dewald related to California. But what had made her run off after she returned to Kansas? And were the two connected?

By the time I opened the pocket doors, the cats strode around examining their home. Both Lady Mittens and Sir Pounce sniffed the surroundings and the furniture to make sure the uncouth intruders were no longer present. I couldn't blame them. They jumped on my lap at the same time and made me a sacred tome to be bookended. Two hands scratched two heads resulting in musical purring. "If all of life could be like this," I thought, but knew it wasn't to be.

Chapter Twelve

It figured to be a busy day. The car would come in handy, although I hated to admit that to King Mar. I would just as likely receive a big warm smile had I acknowledged his generosity. It was good, after all, to let friends know how much you appreciated them.

I visited Don Long first and updated him on where I was so far. I didn't feel it prudent to inform Arlene Nathan just yet regarding the more sensitive nature of my discoveries. Don knew her better and could determine the most judicious course of action.

Don worked third shift and would get home about six or shortly thereafter. I made a quick cup of coffee, fed the cats, and picked up the car. I met him at his place and drove toward Arlene Nathan's home. An awkward silence settled in. Even with the worldly strength he had exhibited, there were a lot of words caught in my mouth as I tried to figure out exactly how to present the salacious info and the possible harm to young Debra Rose Nathan's reputation. In the end, I didn't need to worry.

"I was part of the music scene for quite a while. Been to all kinds of big cities and small towns. So, I've heard stories like that," he replied after I laid out the possibilities. "I suppose every young girl can't be an actress, huh?"

"Would she have done that though?" I asked, hoping

to mitigate the insinuations of it. "I mean, you know her pretty well."

"I thought I knew myself, too. That is, until I started to tour." I didn't have the heart to ask him to dredge up his demons. He made me fully aware he understood them.

We sat there in the car in front of the house. I didn't notice the young man until he was right on top of us. A faint knock at the window, almost apologetic in nature, startled me. Don and I got out of the car. There stood a young boy, maybe eighteen or nineteen, rather tall, approaching six feet, with pale red hair and freckles. He wore a pale yellow short-sleeved shirt and jeans with rolled up cuffs, worn as though he might not have had a lot of options at home. His loping posture reminded me of an Irish version of Jimmy Stewart.

"Hi, Mr. Long."

"Howdy, kid." The young boy nodded, hands still in pockets, and kept his gaze at his feet. "This is Harold Bergman. Mr. Bergman, this is Jeremy Thatcher. He and Debra Rose graduated high school together."

"Hiya, son."

"Sir," he politely responded.

"What can I do for you, kid?"

"Just hoping Debra Rose was around."

Don Long had an almost embarrassed look on his face when he turned to look at me. I imagined the uncertainty of what to say given this was not a police matter but could become one fast. I stepped in with the professionalism the situation needed.

"It seems that Debra Rose has run off again, Jeremy. She got back from California, stayed with her mom for a bit, and then just went missing. You wouldn't have any idea where she might have gone off to?"

He turned white as though he had seen a ghost. He took a step back, and I thought for sure he would faint dead away.

"No, sir. Gee. Wow! I mean, oh my." Don helped Jeremy lean against the car, and the kid buried his face in his hands. He was about ready to collapse from shock.

"How long have you known her, Jeremy?" I tried to get him back on track, thinking about his dear friend with pleasant memories rather than dwell on the possibilities and adolescent mind could dredge up.

"Since grade school. I've had a crush on her just about my whole life."

I leaned down in front of him as though I had a small child in front of me.

"Listen. I'm a private detective. Mr. Long and Debra Rose's mom have asked me to look for her. I swear to you I am going to do my best. You understand?" He looked up at me with tears in his eyes and nodded. "If you think of anything that might help, you let Mr. Long here know. Okay?"

"Yes, sir."

He stood up and straightened himself out before nodding that he was okay, then left on unsteady feet. I looked back at Don.

"The kid's taking it pretty hard."

"When she came back, he thought it was his chance."

"His chance? At what?"

"They were all set to go to the senior prom when he took ill. His mom thought it was strep throat. She kept him from going. Come to find out it wasn't but a head cold."

"He live around here?"

"Down the road a spell."

I thought this Thatcher kid might have a clue where Debra Rose might be, assuming we determined nothing bad about her disappearance. I found it easy to consider the girl finding some comfort from an old friend and trusting him to help her out of a jam. If he had any faith in me, he might eventually warm up to helping out. Until then, I had to stay on track with the information I had so far.

Don stepped inside to visit with Arlene Nathan while I waited outside. I didn't ask him what he told her, and he didn't tell me. I trusted his judgment in this knowing I couldn't be bogged down every time an excessive emotional reaction was a possibility. I took comfort in Proverbs 14:30 "*A sound heart is the life of the flesh: but envy the rottenness of the bones.*"

I dropped off Don at his apartment and then stopped at the main offices of Farmers and Bankers Life Insurance. They weren't too far from where I lived, down around the intersection of First and Market. The thought twirled around my head as to why they weren't willing to pay off if their own investigator thought it was murder. This is where I lacked understanding of business bureaucracy. That had me at a disadvantage. Now I would find out.

The well-dressed gentleman in his mid-forties with a tiny swatch of gray hair right at the ears and a firm handshake greeted me as I entered. He chatted with the efficient-looking secretary when I made my presence known. He introduced himself as Troy Harding and invited me into his office in the same way my Army pals would encourage me to accompany them to the local bar during basic training. I couldn't be certain if his jovial behavior was due to thinking of me as a potential client. I needed to squash that notion quickly.

"Just so I'm up front here, Sharon Kaye has hired me to investigate her husband's death. As you are probably aware she feels her husband had been murdered, likely by an ill-tempered client. I have been in touch with the police about the case."

All the time, Mr. Harding nodded in complete understanding of my recitation. It wasn't dismissive as much as designed to get us to move beyond what we both already knew. A total study in respectful professionalism. It galled me just the same.

"Understandable, especially when one considers the twenty-five-thousand-dollar policy she wants to claim. However, if you have consulted with the police, I am certain you will find their detailed report coincides with our findings as well."

We played chess with vocabulary pieces. I hoped I would be able to get past the opening and toward the middlegame.

"Except that one of your investigators concurs with mine and Mrs. Kaye's assessment."

"Oh?" I had caught him off guard. Maybe another pawn would fall to me. To reach for bigger pieces would take a little more time.

"I encountered Kelly Gardner at the park where they found Mr. Kaye's body. He shared with me his assessment of the case."

He pursed his lips and narrowed his eyes. Even though not directed at me, I could see the palpable anger in his face. He clicked on his intercom.

"Miss Moyer, would you have Mr. Van Sickle come

into my office please?"

His tone was terse and clipped. I imagined Miss Moyer recognized its meaning. I heard a modicum of restraint although my comment had triggered a deep consternation within him.

A full minute of silence followed an affirmation by the secretary. Mr. Harding had no need to explain his recent actions or the reason for requesting Mr. Van Sickle, whoever that might be. When the minute ended, a very tall and slender man came in after a brief knock. Mostly bald, he had a small amount of reddish-brown hair circling his head like a crown, and had eyes like a tired bloodhound. Rolled-up shirt sleeves and a loosened tie with the upper button undone showed he hadn't expected a business meeting.

"Excuse me," he said as he started to roll down his shirt sleeves.

"No need for that, Tom." Despite the relief from Troy Harding, Thomas continued to get himself back into a professional appearance, probably for his co-worker's sake more than mine. "I thought you had told Kelly Gardner to cease and desist all investigatory behavior."

"I did." The response was blank.

"This is Harold Bergman. He is in the employ of Sharon Kaye. He encountered Mr. Gardner in the park, and it was Mr. Gardner who passed along his unsubstantiated belief that Martin Kaye was murdered."

"Oh dear." He looked like Ed Wynn when his two fingers covered his lips.

"Oh dear, indeed." Troy Harding appeared none too pleased. "In my mind, this is cause for termination. As you oversee the adjusters, I will leave it to your discretion. But please ensure an incident like this does not happen again."

"Yes, sir." Thomas Van Sickle had not completely rolled down his sleeves or pulled up his tie. He did leave promptly. Troy Harding gathered himself with a deep breath and slow exhale. I gathered the scene was for my benefit to convince me of an error they did not wish to be a part of or take ownership for.

"Kelly Gardner had been a lawyer, disbarred for various irregularities and ethics violations. Due to confidentiality concerns, I am not at liberty to go into them, but I'm certain it is a matter of public record. However, we considered that his background might make him suitable to work with our adjusters in primarily a research capacity only. He has an amazing capacity for analytics. There have, however, been a few instances where he believed our assessment of a policy claim to be ill-advised. He took it upon himself to, shall we say, examine these independently. Again, without provocation or authorization."

If I didn't know any better, I would have taken this for a prepared speech as though he had just won an Academy Award.

"Mr. Gardner indicated he had information regarding an argument between Mr. Kaye and an unidentified individual as well as other physical evidence."

"This firm is unaware of any such encounter Mr. Kaye might have had nor any other physical evidence not currently in the possession of the Wichita Police Department." His demeanor relaxed from tight-fisted to generous, but certainly not in any humanitarian fashion. His concession was not an admission of liability. "Kelly

Gardner does not represent this firm when it comes to claims resolutions. I am truly sorry for any misinformation this employee provided."

He stood up and extended his hand, a declaration of finality. Farmers and Bankers Life Insurance, in the person of Troy Harding, had formerly decreed this to be the end of discussion in the matter of Martin Kaye. Whether I had any proof of Sharon Kaye's assertion mattered less than the fact I would not accede to a professional brush off. I left Troy Harding with an outstretched hand and an embarrassed expression on his face.

I drove up the street and around the corner and parked the car in the back of the Pan American Café. A couple of the waitresses enjoyed a smoke break out back. They asked if I wanted lunch, and I politely declined. Halfway on the walk home, I regretted my decision as a noticeable growl emanated from my belly. By the time I got home, my two felines exhibited some dismay at an unknown slight. I filled their bowls and got by on two pieces of bread and a slice of cheese.

From my sudden entry, I had overlooked an envelope slid under my door. It was not from Western Union, nor did it have a stamp on it. The paper was a fine vellum with my name in elegant, scripted writing, likely using an old-fashioned fountain pen. A wax seal secured the back. The imprint of the seal appeared to be an eagle clutching feathered arrows. Inside I found an ornate invitation, requesting my presence tomorrow evening at the home of Alan Isbell of 320 North Belmont Place in College Hill, Wichita for a soiree on behalf of the Hephaestus Society, a small group of wealthy contributors to the arts in Wichita, Sedgwick County, and Kansas. I had absolutely no idea why such a group would invite me although I found some appeal to it.

A hand-written note on simple white paper gave me at least the hint of what to expect:

"I would very much like to clear up some misunderstandings regarding recent events on the West Coast. I hope you will accept my hospitality." The signature; A. Isbell.

I had started with Max Burke, a blustering so-called private detective looking for stag photos. It segued into Ralph Dewald, a failed politician with the same capacity for doubletalk insinuating industrial espionage. Now it reached perhaps the highest level. Who knew what Alan Isbell would claim. It started to look like I was Cinderella at the ball.

Chapter Thirteen

Something stuck in my gut about the encounter at the insurance agency, the nature of the industry notwithstanding. Very little came across as businesslike and professional about it. It had the unpleasant odor of a family dispute. Troy Harding appeared far too tight-lipped and standoffish, using carefully worded dialogue written by some lawyer with the firm more concerned with liability than courteous assistance. Thomas Van Sickle acted like the canary had got out of the cage with a cartoonish gulp the only thing missing. From their attitudes toward Kelly Gardner, that just might have been the case. I met the gentleman only once and formed an opinion based on his wardrobe, appearance, and comments. I got the impression they would button him up at work and keep him chained to his desk at a minimum, so if I wanted to get him to open up, I'd have to reach him somewhere he would consider comfortable. Not knowing him, I didn't reckon where that might be.

The Polk directory identified him as residing in some cheap flat on St. Francis between Second and Third Streets. I took a quick walk over there as it was less than a mile away. Unfortunately, my foot throbbed by the time I made it there, likely from the busyness of the day and the lack of rest I provided myself. As with so many other times, I had to muddle through. The dark brick building I came across lacked any refined ornamentation, had several chips on the front porch, and three of the four mailboxes were practically falling off the wall. One of them indicated K Gardner as occupying the ground floor rear apartment. Another example of him stuck in a box.

An aroma reminiscent of old boiled potatoes wafted down from the upper floor, accompanied by the distinct stench of mildew and hopelessness, the last step before the morgue. I stood in front of the thin wooden door and knocked lightly. My sense of courtesy and respect prevented me from a full onslaught. However, after two repetitions of gentility, I used my fist to pound harder and called his name in a desperate tone. I got no response. I didn't expect someone to graciously offer any kind of information for the purpose of getting me to depart, and I had no desire to rap on other doors. Certainly not the potato soup room.

I needed to bring Sharon Kaye up to date with the information I had obtained and perhaps casually reference Kelly Gardner. I hadn't determined from him specifically if he knew her or just conducted an independent investigation of his own volition. My foot really started to throb as I approached Elm Street from Broadway and saw Kelly Gardner emerging from the Commodore with a nervous and antsy look. I dismissed the notion of coincidence at once.

I gave a gentlemanly knock on Sharon Kaye's door. In return, I got a surprised but pleased look from Mrs. Kaye.

"I hope I'm not disturbing you."

"Never, Mr. Bergman." I honestly couldn't tell if a flirtatious tint tinged the comment or it were the exuding of strained pleasantry. Someday, Eileen would teach me such things. For now, I was on my own.

Given my encounter with the gentlemen from the insurance agency, when I walked in, I saw the apartment in a different way, not as though the occupant were a destitute businesswoman in mourning but a bon vivant who experienced a temporary interruption in her luxurious lifestyle. I didn't like to feel that way, but I couldn't help it. It would take great restraint on my part to remember who I had for a client.

That tingle in the back of my head reiterated a sensible suggestion of ending this case. However, to teeter on uncertainty was not a proper excuse to give up. It marked me as unqualified and afraid of failure. From the war, I knew I could not acquiesce.

"Farmers Insurance is being rather steadfast. They are definitely not on your side."

"Who did you talk to there?"

"Troy Harding."

She nodded, reached for a cigarette, lit it, and exhaled a plume of smoke almost defiantly.

"A company man through and through," she said almost spitefully.

"Although, apparently there is one employee who is prone to believe your case."

"Oh? Who would that be?" She acted genuinely surprised. Perhaps Olivia de Havilland would play her in the movie version.

"Kelly Gardner. You know him?"

"No." Another plume of smoke came out, almost like a whale spouting a gush of seawater. "Tell me more about him."

I described my encounter in the park with Gardner where he indicated his belief in her husband's murder. Since he didn't provide any specifics, I couldn't take what he said to be anything more than conjecture. With the agency's official stance firmly enunciated, it became clear they considered him a rogue employee whose commentary would not cut ice or have any bearing in a resolution. In essence, his commentary had no influence on her cause.

"Yes, but if he's able to convince them, wouldn't that carry any weight?" It almost sounded as though she tried to convince me, although I didn't know of what. A tone of desperation seeped out as though I were the key to her success. I couldn't figure out why.

"If he could, my activities are redundant as well as a waste of your money."

"You needn't worry. After all, it is my money to waste, Mr. Bergman."

She started to sound like a spoiled little rich girl who wanted to have her cake and eat it, too. As of now, she was.

"So it is." I stood up and turned to leave. At the door, I turned back to her. "If you do encounter this Kelly Gardner, please see if you can get him to reveal what information he has. It would make my job a lot easier. And certainly help you in the long run."

I closed the door behind me as I left. I wasn't interested in her offering me a cocktail or watching her bat her eyes at me. I strongly considered I should drop the case. Then I recalled Gardner indicated Sharon Kaye would want justice served. Just then, I reflected on Isaiah 1:17 "*Learn to do well; seek judgment, relieve the oppressed, judge the fatherless, plead for the widow.*" Until I learned otherwise, Sharon Kaye played the latter role, and I needed to plead her case. This became, for the moment, a moral imperative and not a personal decision.

A day of being stonewalled got me hungry. I continued down Broadway and went into Garvie's for a chicken salad sandwich and a cup of coffee. The last time I ate there, they had a new cook who put too much mayo in the chicken salad. It practically fell out from between the two slices of bread. The waitress apparently remembered my predicament and made sure to advise him not to replicate the event.

The biggest reason for going there was as much to get off my feet. A dull throb emanated from my ankle just above the instep. I often wondered if the stress, rather than excessive use, caused the pain. Since I wasn't a doctor, I continued to address it as needed.

What reason did Sharon Kaye have to lie about knowing Kelly Gardner? I could only assume she hoped to have multiple agents working on her behalf. She likely hoped to increase her chances of a positive resolution. That idea came out of a sense of desperation. I just couldn't see her in that way. Perhaps Kelly Gardner made a discovery due to his position in the insurance agency, presented overtures in the hope he would receive a slight consideration, and became curtailed by Harding and Van Sickle. He would have had to be extremely bold to approach Sharon Kaye especially after his activities came to the attention of his employer. A chance existed she would slight him, and he could lose his job. The risks seemed to heavily outweigh the reward.

While the chicken salad was not a runny soup, it lacked any discernible flavor. The coffee got me through, and my foot had plenty of time to recover. As I now planned to visit Bradley Wolrebinski, I made a quick grab of the car keys from the Pan American and drove north to his house on Park Place. Sixteen blocks were far too much to bear at this point.

At just about seven p.m., I figured it to be rather early in the evening for my novelist friend who routinely stayed up until one or two in the morning. Luckily, he had not begun to set down for the evening to write. He invited me in and immediately poured two healthy glasses of schnapps. We sat in the parlor where we had passed many nights over a chessboard or in deep conversation. Most of the time I listened as Bradley became engrossed with the sound of his own voice expounding on any given variety of subjects, most of which revolved around him personally. I could never understand how Svetlana put up with him, but I recognized the sincere love and respect between them.

"What do you know about the Hephaestus Club?" I asked.

"Ah, patrons of the arts, mostly for here in Wichita but they have extended their generosity to other nearby communities. Music, painting, sculpture. Not so much in literature."

"So, they're good people?"

"They're scoundrels. You should keep away from them at all costs." At first, I thought he had a grudge due to some slight toward him. When he continued, I understood it had nothing to do with that. "There is only one identifiable member. Alan Isbell. Rich guy with no visible means of support."

"Do rich people usually have one?"

"You remember Albert Whitman?"

"How could I forget?"

"Import and export. Drug dealing. Isbell has got none of the first, so that means he must have a lot of the second."

I looked at him incredulously.

"Is that the writer in you talking?" In essence, I threw out the gauntlet, perhaps being Socratic as well.

"What does your interest lie in this?"

I pulled out the telegram and showed him. He read it over a couple of times as though he were a codebreaker.

"So, *nu*?" I pondered.

"He mentions California. Is this to do with your missing girl?"

"Could be."

"Then you have to go."

"You said they were scoundrels and I should keep away from them at all costs."

"Daniel walked into the lion's den. Daniel walked out. Be like Daniel."

I had never encountered a simpler approach to a difficult encounter. Be like Daniel. I thought of offering that small piece of sage advice to Rabbi Saperstein, but he likely would already know about it.

After more kibbitzing about crime novels and a visit by Svetlana to discuss her new painting project inspired by the pink and orange zinnias she'd planted in her garden, it started to get late. I had absorbed a lot of information in this one day but figured to be no closer to any concrete resolution. Since I still had the car, I decided to try Kelly Gardner's flat one more time.

It didn't seem possible the building could come across as gloomier and more lost, but it did. A complete sunset approached which left a sickening glow over this dilapidated building. The faded odor of boiling potatoes remained and insinuated itself into my memory, a redolence of decay and disuse. There were no lights on outside of a bare light bulb in the main hallway. It created monstrous shadows of unidentifiable beasts. I knocked lightly, almost quietly on Gardner's door. It opened slightly. I pushed my way in, not even considering who might have been on the other side. Certainly not wise for a former policeman.

A newspaper was at the foot of a chair next to a side table with a small lamp, the only light in the room. The outline of a sink full of dishes depressed me as much as the intoxicated look on Kelly Gardner's face. An empty bottle rolled around on the floor and dampened the newspaper with its scant remnants. Two fingers of amber liquid remained in a glass on the table with the lamp.

Gardner looked at me as though he had never seen me before but didn't care about that one way or the other. Whatever he had been in the past, however smart or secure or strong, had all drained away. A clerk with occasional delusions of grandeur. I was certain Troy Harding and Thomas Van Sickle pressed that out of him after learning of his improprieties, leaving him a vague ghostly shell of who he had been up to this point.

"What is there between you and Sharon Kaye?"

"Who?"

His breath was acrid.

"You came out of the Commodore. I saw you."

He plopped down in his chair, grabbed the glass, and polished it off.

"I tried to squeeze her, see if I could make a buck.'

"Off what?"

"Playing her against the agency."

"So, you've got nothing."

He looked up at me desperately.

"Something ain't right. I'm telling you."

When you fall from a great height, you often get squashed. But, sometimes, there is a fragment of credibility that remains. In the park, I met a secretive wanderer. His employer led me to believe he was a stray dog. Based on his appearance tonight, I saw a man on his last legs. And yet I couldn't help but agree with him. If only I knew why.

Chapter Fourteen

I knew I would be making a trip across town to College Hill the next evening, so I took the car back to my apartment to have it readily available. Only one of my neighbors, Elbert Lewis, had a car as well as a telephone. I found enough space in the back of the building for two flivvers to rest. Although, I was certain Mr. Lewis might take exception to that description. He had a brand new shiny black two-door Ford Super Deluxe. The so-called Pounce-mobile could not compare. I had half a mind to bring my car over to the Goodrich-Silverton Filling Station on North St. Francis, not too far from Kelly Gardner's flat. I thought better of when I realized it wouldn't change anyone's mind about me in that part of town. Another of the many reasons why car ownership could be just as much of an issue as not having one.

I thought about having Eileen accompany me. The legitimate part of the Hephaestus Society centered around the arts in Wichita and the region. I knew she would enjoy that given she was more insightful than me in that regard. While I had attended several functions with Bradley and Svetlana in the past, I had a greater appreciation of the art world than an understanding. However, if they were as unsavory as Bradley led me to believe, I didn't want to put her in any kind of danger, whatever kind might present itself. Then again, she was perceptive and smart, on top of which I developed a growing fondness for being with her. I doubted anything execrable would occur at a cocktail party. At least, I hoped so.

Right before breakfast at the King's X, I found a pay phone and called the switchboard at the Beacon. Renee Loomis recognized my voice before I said two words and connected me with Eileen.

"You rang, my liege." Eileen's sense of humor could be variable, based on who she spoke with. She was far more reserved with others.

"How would you like to attend a soiree in College Hill tonight?"

"My soiree dress is still at the cleaners."

"Shame. Free food and drink. A chance to rub elbows with the cognoscenti of the arts in Wichita and Sedgwick County."

"Bergman, is this legit?"

"It's a case."

She allowed a pause to dangle like a piece of yarn in front of a cat. I wasn't certain as to whether the idea repelled her or intrigued her.

"I've never seen you work. What time?"

She made me promise that if it were boring and I finished whatever I needed to do that I would take her to Ciro's for chocolates. I agreed. Certainly the least I could do. What could be more enchanting than sweets for a sweet lady?

While I sopped up my fried eggs with the last of my wheat toast, Max Burke came in to the King's X. If it weren't for his girth, I could have sworn he walked on tiptoes. He was as quiet and deft as Lady Mittens. He looked around him as though an enemy sniper were out there, maybe on top of the Orpheum across the street.

"Any news?" he asked quietly.

"I'm trying to figure out exactly what everyone thinks Debra Rose Nathan has in her possession."

"Like I told you, I thought they were stag photos. I didn't know anything about secret business plans."

"Did you find out anything?"

"No."

"Do you know a Ralph Dewald?"

"No."

"What about Alan Isbell?"

"No. Who are they? LA people?"

"No, local."

"Well, how would I know them?"

I swiveled on my stool and looked at him disapprovingly to where you could practically hear my silent tsk tsk.

"You're supposed to be a detective, Burke." I sighed, then realized dressing him down wouldn't achieve anything. "Do you know who's in charge of the Mellon investigation out there?"

"A Sgt. Jonathan Noone."

"You know him?"

He shrugged. It wasn't an affirmative or a negative. More like ambivalent.

I figured I would have to bite the bullet and spring for a long-distance call to get some real info, assuming this Noone guy would open up to a former police officer with a vested interest in his case. I didn't want Burke to be either a burden or a nuisance, so I instructed him to use his West Coast resources to try to figure out exactly what item Debra Rose Nathan might have had that would have spooked her enough into hiding. If I could get this guy to work for me, it was a sure bet he wouldn't hinder me. Assuming it played out that way.

Don Long had told me Arlene Nathan had switched over to third shift on account of the insomnia that finally took hold of her. Sleepless nights were the symptom of her deep and profound worry and fear. I understood that completely. When I shipped back from Europe, I could almost hear artillery shells in my sleep. I saw mangled bodies and streams of blood in my dreams. Those traumas set me on the path to becoming a private detective. I couldn't save those who had already passed, but maybe I could prevent needless deaths. When it came to Caroline Whitman and Dale Walker, I failed. That only added to the dreams.

Arlene Nathan's front door was open. Through the screen door came a slow plume of smoke. It wasn't until I got up closer that I saw her there with a cigarette in her hand.

"I heard the car," she said. "I don't get too many visitors, and I knew Don had headed home."

"May I come in?"

She nodded and walked away, toward the chair where she took refuge.

"Don switched to first shift to sort of watch over me." She laughed in an ironic sort of way. "I'm rather ashamed to say I probably took the last shift to get away from him." She caught herself appearing embarrassed. "Oh, I don't mean he's a problem or nothing. He means well. Too well."

"Even goodness can be suffocating."

"You either got news or questions." She stared at me in a very perceptive manner. I couldn't be sure where to begin.

After a bit, I cautiously advised her of what I had discovered so far. I told her about Brooks Mellon and Max Burke, referenced what her daughter might have done after the acting gig went downhill. I didn't get into any graphic details. Nor did I bring up the whole industrial espionage aspect, but simply mentioned other people seemed to be looking for her as well. Out of the blue, she asked me the most frightening thing I could imagine.

"You think she's still alive, Mr. Bergman?"

I stared at her as she did with me. I wanted to choose my words carefully, not give in to the temptation of despair but neither wishing to build an idol of false hope. The Golden Calf might be shiny but nothing that could bring true comfort.

"I do. She's got something they want, and they're still buzzing around me figuring I might lead them to her. When it begins to get quiet, that's when I'll start to worry."

"You have a tough job, don't you?"

"How's that, ma'am?"

"You've got to find her before they do as well as protecting her from them. All the while making sure you don't fall into the gutter."

It worked out as me being bait for the trap. Whoever might be involved, whichever faction wanted the brass ring, they all knew I was the point man, out in front digging through the brush in the jungle, clearing a path for them. But they forgot I had a strength more powerful that they could never touch.

Arlene Nathan showed an incredible amount of poise and strength. Her only daughter had her dreams smashed and now found herself among the missing.

Perhaps like Caroline Whitman and Alonzo Washington, Debra Rose had made herself scarce so that a greater evil would not find her. I found out too many times the only way to smash the wicked was to bring them into the light.

As I left her house and started to get into my car, I saw a figure down the road apparently hiding behind a tree. It could have been anyone, a child playing or a hobo passing through. I had the unnerving sense that someone watched me. Rather than try to be deceptive, I strode straight down the road. Finally, the nervous figure proved to be young Jeremy Thatcher.

"It's you, Mr. Bergman. I wondered who might be bothering Mrs. Nathan."

I looked around trying to figure out how he got there, whether he had a car or a bicycle.

"Were you wanting to see Mrs. Nathan?"

"No, sir."

He paused awkwardly. He wasn't going to continue unless I asked.

"Where do you live, Jeremy?"

"Oaklawn area."

"You drive here?"

"No, sir. Walked."

"That must be a good three miles."

"Three and a half. Closer to four."

I looked down at my foot.

"Too much for me."

"How's that?"

I explained to him about my war injury. Even though I walked around town a bit, I found greater comfort in cabs. Of course, now that I had the car at my disposal, it became easier to amble down to this neck of the woods. I tried my best to put him at ease and not make him think he was in any sort of trouble. The kid seemed out of sorts, almost beside himself, like he tried to help and just didn't know how.

"So, why are you here, Jeremy?"

"Just worried is all."

I thanked him for his concern and then just waited for the conversation to peter out after he declined my offer of a ride home. He acted like a good old-fashioned Boy Scout, but a tickle in the back of my neck had me wonder if he had an ulterior motive.

It was just after noon when I got back home. The cats both greeted me with long stretches and rather passive requests for food or attention. With cats, you really can't tell. You offer one and if it doesn't placate them, you offer the other. In the end, it winds up a rather easy conjecture.

Mrs. Cora Peacock in apartment 101 allowed me to use her phone for a long-distance phone call. I assured her I would give her the cash for it as soon as the operator advised me of how much I owed. She was especially grateful to me for keeping the building safe, even though I didn't hold a position as security guard. Our landlady, Constance Hanover, praised me for my forthrightness and conscientiousness. Apparently, that meant I kept everyone safe. With so many folks as residents of longer standing than myself, the building had an almost family-like feel to it.

It only took five minutes for the local operator to connect me to one in Los Angeles and another three minutes for the switchboard at police headquarters to locate Sgt. Jonathan Noone. He sounded as young as me, very upbeat for a homicide detective, almost too eager. I didn't have trouble convincing him of my intentions.

"Brooks Mellon was a creepy guy who had his fingers in a variety of pies. But I'm sure you already know that."

"You have any leads on his murder?"

He sighed. I recognized the sound of it. It meant you tried your hardest but ran into a lot of dead ends. The kind of people Brooks Mellon would associate with were not particularly interested in cooperating with the police. Given the nature of the victim, they likely figured on one less arrest to make in the future. But you had to keep trying for the sake of your professional integrity.

"A few, but they're not panning out. Most of his so-called models are scared young girls with no incentive to come forth. His customers are scared middle-aged married men with every reason to stay away from this mess. And the ones we've got tagged as the money men are keeping their mouths shut and lawyering up, even though we don't have a thing on them."

"Is there any way of telling what may have been taken from his studio? If I knew that, I might be able to figure who exactly is chasing this girl here. It might lead back to your killer."

"We're still going through the inventory. He didn't keep the most meticulous records. Not that a guy like him is the biggest accounting hound."

"What do you know about Max Burke?"

"If you come across that fella, tell him he isn't going to be welcome back here."

I needed no elaboration on that. I asked Noone to keep me updated with any updates by leaving a message for Clarence Mendenhall at the Wichita Police Department. Overall, it turned out to be a pleasant conversation that regrettably yielded nothing new.

I gave Mrs. Peacock a ten-dollar bill after the long-distance operator advised me the charges were a bit over eight dollars. Mrs. Peacock, in return, gave me a loaf of oatmeal raisin bread she had baked that morning. I considered it a rather fair exchange.

I thought I could use a quick nap before changing and picking up Eileen, so I lay in my bed captivated by the sounds of two cats purring on either side of me. It wasn't that blissful noise that kept me awake. Rather the thought that a young girl from Kansas, hoping to fulfill a dream, stepped into the mire of a sinister world. When she tried to leave it behind, it followed her like a harpy. As of now, the shadows had swallowed her up.

While it had the makings of a melodrama on stage, it occurred to me that I had a lot in common with Debra Rose Nathan. Pearl Harbor instilled a passion in me that demanded I raise a flag and defend my country. While I might have thought police work would prepare me for the instruments of war, I had witnessed atrocities and death of a magnitude unknown to me before. I got shot and went through a long recovery, but those were just the physical manifestations. The injury was deeper and inaccessible.

Fortunately, I had my father and rabbi as well as friends in the police department. Debra Rose Nathan had a desperate but ill-equipped mother and a weary former jazz musician. Perhaps a freckled young boy. If I were fortunate enough to find her, the real recovery would take a lot longer than even mine.

Chapter Fifteen

What do you wear to an arts-related soiree in one of the finer neighborhoods in Wichita? I could ask that question, aloud or in my head, as often as possible and still not come up with an answer. There were no fashion magazines like *Glamour*, *Bazaar*, or *Vogue* readily available to me to provide an answer. I owned a Bible with Masoretic text and a few *True Detective* and *Dime Detective* magazines. Perhaps I needed to think of it as my bar mitzvah, then realized there was nothing overtly religious about this affair. Besides, that solemn event wasn't remotely artistic, unless I considered my cousin David's brand new tallis. I chose a dark blue suit, pale gray shirt with a silver tie, and my black brogues. Additionally, I found a gold tie tack that seemed to add a certain *je ne sais quoi*. Even when I fought in France, I never had that.

When I picked up Eileen, I realized I had taken her for granted all these years. She wore a sage and pale-yellow off-the-shoulder sun dress. White woven sandals with a small heel and ankle straps lifted her into the status of elegance. A simple gold chain with a butterfly ornament hung gracefully around her neck. The pale pink lipstick accentuated her mouth and jawline. She put Veronica Lake to shame. My jaw was agape, and I stood silent for about thirty seconds.

"Why haven't I swept you off your feet before?"

"Well, I've been wondering the same thing," she replied with a sigh. For the life of me, I couldn't tell if that came out as comic timing or serious regret. It would require greater consideration at a more appropriate time.

On the drive over, I filled her in on the case in a kind of abbreviated detail. Debra Rose Nathan's disappearance had set me off on a chase for an unknown item stolen from a sleazy photographer's studio. One person thought it was stag photos. Someone else claimed they were industrial plans. Apparently, the vastly wealthy Alan Isbell, head of the Hephaestus Society, might have had further information which he graciously invited me to learn. Why he would take me into his confidence was completely undetermined at this moment.

"I don't know who's telling the truth," I finally said, "and I don't really care. My only interest is to find the girl."

"That makes sense. What do you want me to do?"

"You don't have to do anything per se. This is just my way of taking you on a cheap date with delicious grub and free booze at a swank joint in town." She smacked me on the arm. I made sure to keep my hands on the steering wheel. "Hey."

"I'm not just another pretty face."

"But you do have a pretty face."

"Thank you for noticing. But since I will be with you and you filled me in on all this stuff, I might as well help as best I can."

"Well, for the moment, just keep your eyes and ears open. Make a note of people you meet or see. Anything interesting or off-putting that someone says. Later, you can tell me what you think of how they looked and if you heard something that could be interpreted differently."

She agreed with her assignment since it didn't involve any danger. Although I got the impression she might have been disappointed by that.

Alan Isbell's home on Belmont Place turned out to be far more fabulous than the quaint Tudor home in Eastborough of the late Arthur Whitman. The various peaks throughout resembled turrets. The house sat back from the street and a stone archway stood at the entrance to the walkway leading to the house. Only the Campbell Castle in Riverside had more opulence. And we hadn't yet stepped inside. The man who lived here exuded elegance, wealth, and a desire to keep apart from the hoi polloi. Unless, of course, he invited them directly.

As I hoped to be able to leave easily, I parked on the street out front, went around to the passenger door, and opened it for Eileen. It was my intention to convince her of my gentlemanly charms. By now, she either accepted them as fact or she didn't. I imagined she did.

We felt as though we were gliding down the walkway. It had less to do with what we wore and where we went and more about who I was with. For as long as I'd known Eileen Horowitz, I had never been so at ease with her as I did right then. I had to shake the notion out of my head as we approached the door and remember I was on a case. I realized it could be far too easy to get distracted.

The man who opened the door did not appear to be a butler in the strictest sense. More like a concierge. He collected my invitation, glanced at it, and admitted us without so much as a wave of his arm. A suave gentleman with brushed back silver-gray hair and a thin moustache turned in our direction. He wore a tuxedo finer than any I had ever seen before, not that I had many occasions to experience tuxedos or cared to in the future. A very tall man stood next to him. His physique reminded me either of Bronco Nagurski or Mount Everest. I sensed a striking familiarity to him that I couldn't quite place. Since they stood in the center of the foyer and greeted everyone who passed, I took the man in the tuxedo to be our host. The taller guy might have been the pastry chef for all I knew.

"Mr. Bergman." He extended his hand and grasped mine firmly, in a welcoming and friendly gesture as opposed to oppressive, which might have come later. "I'm Alan Isbell."

"It is a distinct pleasure, Mr. Isbell. May I introduce Miss Eileen Horowitz."

Even though he was the furthest thing from European, he took Eileen's hand and kissed it in that fashion. Eileen appeared impressed but cautious.

"The pleasure is all mine, Miss Horowitz." After a brief fixation, he stood tall and turned toward the large creature behind him. "And this is my associate, Zachary Molloy."

Finally, a bell rang. "Associate" would have been the last word that came to my mind when I considered Zach Molloy. I had a few run-ins with him as a beat cop back in the late 1930s. He was rumored to have fled Chicago when the gangs broke up after Capone's arrest on tax evasion. No one could confirm the stories, but they were certainly useful in creating a certain type of aura. There were claims he killed at least five men back then. I had never heard of Alan Isbell until recently, but Zach Molloy was a sly and sinister man. This affiliation at first appeared to be between odd bedfellows. Without knowing much about Alan Isbell, I might be wrong.

"I'm both surprised and honored by the invitation." I didn't mind playing a lackey since I was in Isbell's home at his request. He would get around to business at his leisure. I didn't have to wait long.

"Zachary, please make sure you offer Miss Horowitz some refreshments. Introduce her to that Italian artist we have this evening. I am sure she would be quite charmed by him and his *aeropittura*."

Eileen and I exchanged glances. I wondered whether she understood. She did. She made sure I was not worried. I wasn't.

Alan Isbell walked briskly toward a large oak door just off the foyer. I guessed it to be a private library of some sort, which proved correct. We entered, and the door closed behind me with a soft thud. I had the strange sensation of a cave deep in the desert. The door must have been so thick as to drown out sounds from beyond. Only the sound of my heart starting to beat just a little faster filled the dull emptiness in my ears. I feared no man, but I understood what most were capable of.

He poured a brandy in an elegant snifter and handed it to me. I wasn't as much of a rube as anyone might think. I held the glass properly and swirled the liquid around as I tried to get it to an acceptable temperature. He did as well, brought the glass up to his nose, and inhaled as though it gave him life.

"Remy Martin Louis Treize. Prewar." He said it proudly as though he referred to his children.

"I'm more the Manischewitz type."

I could have enjoyed all the pretenses of the civilized trappings of the rich and taken advantage of the opportunity. But I was not there as a patron of the arts nor a potential benefactor. My impatience came out more like vaudeville shtick.

"So am I. Just another member of the tribe."

Typically, people made a big deal of my being Jewish because they had limited experience with them. Alan Isbell seemed to play on our mutual sympathies and shared heritage as he emphasized the façade often required by Jews to wear. He sat down in a winged back leather chair. He held out his hand toward the companion beside it.

"I am aware"—he spoke softly—"of a Max Burke who has accosted you regarding merchandise stolen from a photographer in Los Angeles."

"I'm not going to insult your intelligence by asking how you know. But I am interested in discerning how it involves you."

"The photographer in question, Brooks Mellon, was, among other things, a straw man for our arts group. He planned to buy various pieces of art that we would be able to use toward the endowment of the Wichita Art Museum. I am a dear friend of Mrs. Elizabeth Stubblefield Navas. Mr. Mellon had photographs of various paintings and sculptures and had planned to send them to us to determine what we wished him to buy. Naturally, his death is quite disconcerting."

"Especially for him," I commented. The dissertation got as biting as the brandy. He presented himself as Laurence Olivier in Henry V while I did my best Fred Allen.

"Yes, well, now we no longer have a straw man and these works of art, which could have been purchased rather cheaply, are out of our reach, both physically and economically."

"With regard to Mr. Mellon, you said 'among other things' relating to his business dealings. Were you aware of what they were?"

"To a certain extent. But our position was if we didn't ask, he didn't have to tell."

"So, your involvement pertained solely to art acquisitions?"

"Precisely."

"Why did Burke think they were stag photos?"

"Because he's a cheap gumshoe out for a quick buck." Isbell's retort had more of a sting filled with venom or a hypodermic filled with dope. Almost as though his contempt was on full display. He caught himself and settled back down. The slight redness in his face returned to pale white.

"I assume you have a suggestion of some sort?"

"Continue on with your admirable career and disregard this Hollywood flatfoot."

"Probably a wonderful idea."

I guzzled down his French booze like grape Nehi and let out a satisfied sigh. I didn't wait for an escort. I simply got up and left the room without so much as a handshake upon my departure. In the larger parlor across from the main foyer, I found Eileen talking to a smartly dressed woman who looked more like an accountant than a patron of the arts. She appeared perhaps in her late forties and wore tortoiseshell horn-rimmed glasses that gave her a Dorothy McGuire look. She had on a gray suit, pulled in at the waist that accentuated her bosom. Eileen glanced at me glancing.

"Harold, you've got to meet this absolutely charming woman." Eileen's voice dripped with sugar. "Dorothy Martin, this is Harold Bergman. Harold,

Dorothy Martin."

Dorothy Martin had a pleasant smile but not nearly as elegant as how she appeared. She came across as distracted, her gaze darted around the room and only occasionally fell back to Eileen and me. She was either searching, watching, or waiting.

"And what is it you do, Miss Martin?" I inquired.

"Mrs. I'm widowed."

"My apologies."

"No need. I'm the curator of a small gallery in Pittsburgh along the Allegheny River. I travel quite a bit purchasing art pieces for sale to some of my more, shall we say, established collectors."

"Sounds fascinating."

"So does this Hephaestus Society. Since you're a local resident as well as a private detective as Miss Horowitz has described, what do you know about them? Is Mr. Isbell a reliable man to do business with?"

The question caught me off guard, so far from expected I couldn't quite grasp the connection or the intent. Art collectors and gallery curators acted like members of the OSS. Paintings and sculpture as a refined cover for a deeper and likely more wicked plan. The exalted air of the affluent made me dizzy. I was out of my league, and I knew it.

"Unfortunately, I just met Mr. Isbell tonight. I wouldn't be much use with an assessment of his professional integrity."

"I'm sure I'll find out once we start negotiating prices."

It seemed she referenced business tactics, but I had an inkling of an intention beyond her stated business. I smiled and excused us from her bobbing head and wandering eye. At the far end of the room, I caught Zach Molloy track my movements. Bradley had the right notion about Daniel in the lion's den. Faith and urgency would extricate me.

"Have you had a nosh?" I whispered in Eileen's ear.

"The cucumber sandwiches are outstanding, darling," she responded mockingly.

"Time to leave."

As we made our way through the gathering, I saw Ralph Dewald talk with Alan Isbell just inside the library. He saw me notice him and shut the door. To stag films and industrial plans, I could add works of art to the mound of lies. This turned into a Tower of Babel. At some point, it would be struck down.

Chapter Sixteen

Brown's Grill and Cafeteria on North Hillside opened just last March. They proclaimed themselves as "The House of Cleanliness" and attracted staff from Wesley Medical Center just across the street as well as the University of Wichita. You had to assume that doctors, nurses, and professors were a higher class of clientele. At least, that was what the owner, Dick Brown, expected. I hoped our being there did not lower their standards.

Eileen sat in wonder with mouth agape and watched me devour my hamburger as I washed it down with coffee. When I finally looked up, I wondered what exactly I had done to warrant a look of confusion mixed with amazement. She had put down her grilled cheese sandwich in order to analyze my frenzied behavior. Since her social experience with me was limited over the last several years, she had a reason to wonder.

"Are you that hungry?" she asked.

"I'm confused." Her look was one of passive encouragement. I put my burger down, wiped my hands and face, and crossed my hands in front of me. "I expected Alan Isbell to be evasive, not straightforward, slightly condescending, and almost threatening. I expected Zach Molloy to be intimidating and gruff, not reserved and patient. But to discover Ralph Dewald at an art group's social gathering made no sense at all. He probably thinks Burma Shave signs are Shakespearean sonnets. On top of which, what does any of this have to do with Debra Rose Nathan? There was no mention of her or film or anything taken from Mellon's studio. Almost as if the item had no importance and the girl's disappearance never occurred."

"You're the detective."

I smiled my sarcastic thanks at her revelation of the obvious.

"Tell me about this Dorothy Martin."

"Well, she was rather droll at first. Despite her association with the arts, she didn't seem the type to be comfortable in a social setting which surprised me. I thought most artsy types enjoyed those kinds of shindigs. But when I mentioned I was there with you, she perked up."

"Does she know me?"

"I don't think so. I just mentioned you were a private detective is all."

Someone did not become aroused by such a profession unless they needed your assistance or were concerned you might be after them and made some impact in their dealings. I had no idea how a gallery curator from Pittsburgh fit into either scenario. She was an appropriate guest at a gathering of the Hephaestus Society but a stranger in a strange land when it came to stag photos or industrial plans. While she did inquire about Isbell's integrity, she offered no reassurance about her own. I fell into a swirl of multiple stories and possibilities none of which led in a straight line to the answer.

Out of the blue, I recalled Proverbs 25:2 "*It is the glory of God to conceal a thing: But the honour of kings is to search out a matter*." I considered myself neither regal nor honorable at that moment. A young girl had gone missing, and I found a game among the wealthy and powerful. Again. Some things never changed.

A surge of pride enveloped me as I watched Eileen daintily eat her sandwich and sip her tea. She had not been put off by the strange woman we encountered or alarmed at my bizarre response to the evening. We had a certain infatuation back in our school days, but it was based on mutual backgrounds and her snappy retorts which made me smile more often than not. Now I saw her as a strong advocate. Nevertheless, I could not ask her to join me any further on this venture. The stakes were too high and the risk too great. Whatever grew between us, I cared enough about her safety to push back a bit.

She declined an offer of a sweet treat at Candyland and feigned being tired from all the excitement. We were quiet on the way back to her apartment. I turned off the engine and started to get out to open the door for me when she touched my arm and turned in her seat toward me.

"Can I tell you something?" she asked softly.

"Sure."

"When you came back from the war, I got a little worried about you. Oh, not because of your injury. You weren't that good of a dancer to begin with."

"Thanks."

"Don't mention it. My concern was that you might go back to the police department."

"You know, this is not any more dangerous than being a soldier."

"Maybe. But in war there is basically just one

enemy. After tonight I realized out here, well, there are so many kinds. You can't tell who your friends are these days."

While I appreciated the sentiment, I didn't want to get into an extended discussion on my views of friendship.

"Would you have rather I became a rabbi?"

She thought about that for a moment. I might have been more appealing to her parents as a suitor with such a noble position. Eileen and I were past that.

"I think what you're doing is fine. It suits you. I guess you need the kind of drive and determination that you've got to be a detective."

"I appreciate that."

"But is there any future in it?"

The question seemed to drop on my head like Newton's apple. Certainly, I was caught up in the need to find a missing girl and focused almost entirely on that case as it existed now. I couldn't quite make out what Eileen tried to get at as she referenced events that had not yet happened. My only recourse was to smile warmly. The answer would eventually occur to me.

I got out of the car, opened her door, and walked her to the front steps. This time, she leaned in for a kiss, not as soft as in the past but not nearly as passionate as I knew she was capable of. When she finished, she went into her apartment building and didn't look back. I watched as she disappeared into the comfortable and safe. It put me at ease.

The car had turned into a useful tool. I had a notion to just park it in the back alley but hesitated to do so before I discussed it with Mrs. Hanover. After I left the Pan American's back area, I started a slow and meticulous walk home. While Eileen hadn't specifically cautioned me about my eating habits, the indigestion percolated in my belly as a reminder. The sounds that emanated from my stomach were not nearly as appealing as that of a purring cat. I hoped I had a Bromo Seltzer at home.

The slow hum of an engine caught my attention. I didn't think to speed up and walk past it. All I could do was turn and face the driver. Max Burke hunkered down behind the wheel, his girth unable to be completely hidden by anything smaller than a Sherman tank. He leaned over to the passenger door and beckoned me in. I sat uncomfortably while this sweaty man looked every which way as he drove the few blocks in the direction of my home.

"That Mickey Dowell is looking for me."

"So? Didn't you pay him to strongarm me?"

"Strongarm? No."

"Okay, whatever you say." He was noncommittal. "Fine. He's looking for you. What does that mean?"

Burke stopped the car in front of my place. I could smell the beer and pickles on his breath. Combined with my growing indigestion, it almost caused me to vomit.

"The front desk clerk at the hotel I'm staying at gives me a message. From Mickey. Says a guy wants to meet with me."

"What guy?"

"I don't know."

"Say, what kind of detective are you?"

"I'm pretty big out in Los Angeles."

"Well, maybe you better head on back there."

"No dice, chum. There's something going on with whatever that chippy stole from Brooks Mellon."

That was the second time he referred to Debra Rose in that fashion. Maybe it was the kind of expression they threw about in Hollywood land, but here in the Great Plains you'd have to be far more wayward and debauched to earn that comment. He already annoyed me with his attitude and lack of professionalism. To refer to a scared kid like that set me off.

"We don't play the same way out here in the plains, Burke. You're nothing but a two-bit grifter looking out for a quick buck. From what I've seen of you so far, you'll get squashed like a bug and not even know it when it happens. You have no idea who you are up against."

Neither did I for that matter, but it just came out of my mouth. I got out of the car, slammed the door, walked off, and didn't turn back until his car screeched away from the curb. I knew I hadn't seen the last of him. The notion of a quick buck would keep him moving ever forward.

The shadowy figure that stood on my front stoop turned out to be none other than Clarence Mendenhall. He pushed his hat back from his forehead in his typical fashion and let out a whistle. He looked in the direction of the vehicle that had just left.

"I hope that wasn't a client of yours," he said emphatically.

"Why is that?"

"With that attitude, I don't think you're gonna get paid."

I smirked at his attempt to restore vaudeville.

"What are you wanting from me?"

"Coroner came back with a report from the autopsy of that Martin Kaye."

"I thought you guys had it down as a suicide."

"Well, we did. But given the uncertainty from the initial report, they conducted an autopsy just to be sure."

I didn't get the impression there had been any uncertainty. Case opened, investigated, file closed. I suspected they had some concerns they did not feel comfortable sharing with anyone, me included. Who knew if Sharon Kaye or even I had caused a few other heads to be scratched.

We stood there and stared at each other. This was an act I experienced with Mendenhall many times before. He wasn't always forthcoming and often made me act like a dentist and pull teeth to keep the conversation going.

"And what, pray tell, did the coroner find?"

"Paraldehyde. Enough to choke a horse."

"Did he intentionally ingest it?"

He shrugged his shoulders.

"If he didn't," he continued, "and someone poured it into that bottle we found—"

"Then that would make it murder," I said to complete the thought.

He squared his hat back up on his head and strode off. This time, he made no final comment on my return to the department. He had said his piece and left me to determine what would be best.

The cats were rather sedate when I came in. I got a can of wet food from the pantry and doled it out into two bowls. Sir Pounce acted like a wanderer in the desert who had a ravenous hunger. Lady Mittens sniffed, walked around the bowl twice, before she finally ate as sweetly as Eileen nibbled at her grilled cheese sandwich. I snickered at how I just compared my two cats to myself and a lovely young lady.

I thought it highly unlikely Kelly Gardner had any notion of the possibility of poisoning. Unless, of course, he was the one who loaded Martin Kaye's bottle of booze. If he had, it would be unlikely he would put me in the direction of murder. I considered Sharon Kaye could have done it. Again, her insistence that her husband's death was murder, hiring me to investigate, only to be the perpetrator was a fantastical notion that bordered on the improbable. If she thought she could get away with it and collect on the insurance money, it might be a viable possibility.

I sat down at the edge of my bed while the cats rewarded me for a late-night meal with some soft purring and butting of their heads against my thighs. Lady Mittens was so exceedingly grateful she climbed onto my lap, up on my chest, and nuzzled my chin. It became the peaceful moment of my day.

A hot bath helped me unwind from the uncertainty and confusion of the evening. Difficulties typically arise when there is not enough information. In this case, I had too much. A jungle of facts and anecdotes, possibilities and speculation. It needed pruning. As the steam rose in my tub, one comment from the Talmud shone in my face like a bright neon sign:

"We do not see things as they are. We see things as we are."

Chapter Seventeen

Until now, I had met with Sharon Kaye in her apartment at the Commodore. It allowed her to be comfortable in her environment and in control of the situation regardless of what it might have been. She always presented herself as well-dressed, poised, with an answer to every question right when asked. I needed to make sure here responses did not come across as planned or rehearsed. I found the way people reveal their true selves is when they are ill at ease and in an unfamiliar place. This is where I could be in control for a change.

I invited her for coffee at the Pan American. It wasn't too far from her but still the place where I felt most relaxed as far as public settings went. The back booth afforded the semblance of privacy and an easy exit out the back through the kitchen if we needed. I knew it was necessary to do all I could to get her to feel safe. I needed to prove my discretion as well as my sincerity.

She walked in with a confident stride just past eleven that Saturday morning. As she moved through the restaurant to look for me, I saw bits of her strength start to melt. The apartment was a sanctuary. In the real world, there were fewer places to hide.

As soon as she sat, I signaled for the waiter to bring coffee. In the meantime, King Mar meandered around the restaurant, chatted with the couple of patrons there for breakfast, but still kept an eye in my direction as I asked him to.

"I have additional information," I started after the coffee arrived, "that your husband may have been poisoned." An inaudible gasp emerged, almost bordering on melodrama, but she said nothing. "First, can you tell me if he was currently in treatment for alcoholism.'

"Well, not treatment per se." Just a few words but they came out haltingly. It is rather difficult to stop a bullet once you pull the trigger.

"Can you elaborate, please?"

"When we were successful, Martin would, well, celebrate. When there was a turn in the market, he would, shall we say, comfort himself. Naturally, in this business, there is a lot of both. At times, one right after the other, back and forth. Therefore, he took to the bottle far more than I thought to be necessary for either occasion. Why do you ask?"

I ignored her question.

"Did he have a doctor in town that he saw on a regular basis? A general practitioner or specialist perhaps?"

"I'm not certain."

"You're not certain?" I retorted quickly, not intent on letting the conversation lag and allow her time to find an appropriate response.

"No, well, maybe there was someone."

"Who?"

"I can't be certain."

I made absolutely sure what I said next came across as pointed and direct. She had to understand the seriousness of my purposes. Her response would either persuade me of her intentions or her duplicity.

"Mrs. Kaye, for me to proceed with this

investigation based on this newly acquired information, it is imperative I get complete and honest answers to these vital questions. Now, was your husband visiting any doctor or any facility in town for the treatment of alcoholism?"

"The Friendly Fever Clinic." She didn't blurt it out; nevertheless, she did utter it forcefully, as though gas escaped from a floating dirigible. Fortunately, she didn't explode. "Most of the towns we lived in, Martin found someone who could help him keep his urges in control. Mind you, he was never diagnosed as being an alcoholic. But he didn't let on to anyone, especially clients, that he likely was. It would have completely ruined us. The folks at the clinic offered him homeopathic treatments. The other stuff made him nervous and irritable. Sometimes even headaches so bad he couldn't move."

She spoke tentatively. Perhaps she might have been ashamed of her late husband's condition or another aspect of his personality. It struck me that she still acted as though she were in complete control. I hadn't rattled her in any fashion.

"Was it paraldehyde he had taken in the past?"

"Yes. That was it."

"Who was the primary doctor he saw?"

"Dr. Richter. Clarence Richter."

I reached across the table and held her clasped hands. Unless or until I knew otherwise, she was my client and deserved my best efforts. Whether I believed in her or trusted her. I didn't let her see my smile. Dr. Richter was a member of Ahavat Achim Hebrew Congregation. A lantzman.

After I saw Sharon Kaye off, I flagged down Richie and had him drive me over to Dr. Richter's house. I remembered I visited there once with my parents around the High Holidays while still in high school. His home befitted a successful member of the medical profession and a righteous member of the temple. Therefore, my tone was completely deferential especially as I bothered him on a Saturday morning.

"It is quite all right, Harold. So, tell me, is this to do with the temple or one of your own affairs?" As with many of the older folks in temple, my current career was not looked upon with any sense of dignity or respectability. I had become the real-life version of seedy little men in overcoats, ironic since I never wore one. It was pointless to convince anyone otherwise.

"Sharon Kaye is my client. I believe her late husband, Martin, might have been a patient of yours recently."

"He consulted with the clinic regarding his drinking habit."

"Did you prescribe paraldehyde?"

The warmth of his face was almost fatherly, but it also had a smidgen of condescension.

"I'm certain you're aware I can't discuss any details to do with a patient of ours."

"Former patient considering he is deceased. A man who has no need of secrecy or privacy any further." I might have come across as too harsh. I didn't care. However, I maintained a professional demeanor complete with a solid unflinching smile. "If you absolutely require a release from his widow, I'm quite certain I can obtain one. But I hope you won't make me go through all of that when a little bit of information would be a mitzvah."

We had gone from parrying based on disrespect for

each other's profession to tacit courtesy and finally to spiritual obligations. There weren't many occasions when I had to duke it out with a fellow Jew. Perhaps many underestimated me based solely on my lack of attendance in shul. How could they know I was an inveterate reader of Torah and Talmud?

"We advocated for diathermy and other homeopathic solutions to provide Mr. Kaye with a greater degree of control in his life. We theorized it would reduce his needs. He, instead, preferred a less than holistic approach and requested we prescribe paraldehyde."

He kept his chin up. Though I had bested him, he insisted on maintaining his pride.

"I take it he was familiar with paraldehyde?"

"Yes. He showed us expired prescriptions from various physicians around the country. Places where he lived previously."

"Would your treatments have helped more than the paraldehyde?"

At this point, I thought of Dr. Richter as a trainer in Kentucky with an inquiry about a thoroughbred or the manager of the next heavyweight champion.

"Absolutely. Our approach does not include substituting one drug for another. By focusing on the body's own natural resources, we can eliminate many maladies that traditional medicine believes can only be cured through chemical therapies."

I allowed him his recitation which amounted to little more than justification bordering on an acute marketing campaign. Perhaps if I saw him at Shabbat services, we would be more inclined for reconciliation. Right now, I had all I needed. I offered a polite and respectful thanks.

Since I used the car more frequently, I hadn't seen much of Richie. I asked him to take me down to visit Arlene Nathan and Donald Long. It would give me the opportunity to check up on his well-being. His asthma hadn't gotten any worse, but he hadn't felt as energized much these days. We were fast approaching summer, and his allergies could subside. He worked fewer hours on account of his more frequent malaise and thought of a move to Colorado where he heard the mountain air was therapeutic. I think he confused all of that with tuberculosis.

When we got down to Arlene Nathan's house, Jeremy Thatcher sat alongside her on the porch and chatted quietly. He appeared to get Arlene to laugh a bit. It was perhaps the first good feelings she'd had since her daughter's disappearance.

"Mr. Bergman, you know Jeremy, right?"

"Yes, ma'am. How are you doing, kid?"

"Just fine, sir. I figured I didn't have much to do today so I'd see if I couldn't brighten up Mrs. Nathan's day a spell."

She smiled.

"And he has."

Along about then, Donald Long with his short shuffling steps came on over.

"I need to have a word with you two."

It wasn't my intention to ignore Jeremy so much as making it clear this was grown up conversation and pretty serious at that. I leaned over and whispered to Richie to talk with the kid and keep him company as well as pay attention to what he said. Richie loved the opportunity to feel like he was a part of my cases.

Inside the house, I sat opposite Mrs. Nathan while

Don Long stood behind me. I ran through my encounters of the previous evening and identified all the players in the scene. Neither Arlene nor Don had heard of any of them. They obviously didn't exist within the same social circles. I experienced a moment of desperation which I didn't mean to allow to come through. It just didn't make any sense how young Debra Rose could be caught up in any of that, even with the possibility of her possessing an item of importance.

"Do you think she's dead, Mr. Bergman?"

The first time she asked if I thought Debra Rose was alive. This time she phrased it as a negative. Arlene Nathan's question came at me straightforward without an ounce of emotion. Just like someone asking about what was for dinner that night. While I wasn't enthused about my progress, I hadn't any dark thoughts creep into my mind.

"No, ma'am, I don't. Whatever is going on, whatever your daughter has fallen into might be criminal in nature, but I do not believe these people are murderers." When I stopped right then, it was almost like I told tales out of *The Wizard of Oz*. Unfortunately, that sounded a mite too reassuring with a touch of rose-colored glasses to it. "That doesn't mean," I continued as seriously as possible, "they are not capable of murder. Let's hope I can figure it out before long."

I stood up to leave. Arlene Nathan grabbed my hand and held me for just a moment.

"Thank you." There were tears in her eyes. I patted Don's arm on the way out.

Richie made his goodbyes with Jeremy, and then he brought me home. On the way, he seemed rather jovial.

"That there is a good kid," he said offhanded.

"Oh? Why do you say that?"

"Well, seems he's had a crush on that girl for years. He was real torn up when she went to California but mighty pleased when she returned. He's real worried, Hirsch. You gotta do what you can to find her."

"I am, Richie." I waited a moment. "So, what else did you two talk about?"

"Cracker Jacks."

"Excuse me?"

"We both collect Cracker Jack prizes and Cracker Jack baseball cards. Of course, I stopped collecting them years ago. He still does though. Loves collecting them."

"You think he knows where Debra Rose is? Maybe, she got scared in California and she wanted him to protect her, hide her from someone?"

Richie appeared pleased I consulted him and took interest in his opinion. He may not have had a lot of book learning but driving a hack taught him about human nature.

As far as Richie could tell, Jeremy might have wanted to be a knight in shining armor, but he didn't have the wherewithal. He was, after all, just a skinny freckled kid with not much going for him. I appreciated his analysis. For me, it was one less person to worry about.

I got off at the cab stand near Douglas and Main. It turned out to be a pleasant day, very little wind, and the sun shone through puffy white clouds. Some fresh air would clear my mind.

We do not see things as they are. We see things as we are.

The words resonated in my mind. Why did these two cases come across as confused conundrums? They were mixed up with too many possibilities. It finally dawned on me I became a Rube Goldberg machine, an amalgamation of conflicted beliefs and ideals, someone who eschewed both sides and chose to sink in the middle without any real sense of clarity. For me to proceed, to locate Debra Rose Nathan, to determine how and why Martin Kaye died, I would need to clear up the angst that had slowly crept into my life.

On top of that, I needed to sort out my true feelings for Eileen Horowitz.

Chapter Eighteen

I was sure Max Burke didn't tell me every bit he knew. Sure, he came across as a low class grifter, a guy who would sell his own mother if it meant an easy buck. Guys like that were likely a dime a dozen in California, especially Los Angeles, and most certainly Hollywood. That kind wasn't as commonplace in these parts. I figured you'd have to be a sweet talker with a small amount of brains to get by in that type of crowd. But I saw right through him from the beginning. That might mean he played a different angle and allowed me to consider him as insignificant while he went about his business. Whatever that really might be.

I knew I had to confront him, since I drew blanks on my own. It was a tough pill to swallow. I had to acquiesce to a guy playing a stooge who tried to pull the wool over on me. At this juncture, I had few other options. He checked out of the Manhattan Hotel and had taken a room in the Lexington Hotel on South Emporia. It was in the vicinity of Lenders Loans, United Finance Corporation, Ross Seed, and the Surf Lounge. A cornucopia fit for his type. I used an angry tone to get the desk clerk to give me Burke's room number. I strode up the stairs irritably and pounded on his door. Strangely, I came across like one of those tough guy movie detectives. It wasn't my style, and I regretted almost immediately how I acted. I realized it was just an act.

Burke opened the door with a start. He appeared to be ready for a tussle, then saw me, and relaxed as though he didn't consider me much of a threat. A condescending smile played about on his face.

"We need to talk," I said bluntly.

"Sure. Over a drink."

"Fine."

He closed the door behind him and gallantly allowed me to lead the way. I thought better and stood aside for him. He tipped his cap to the desk clerk. I imagined Burke had tipped the guy for booze or girls. We were side by side just outside the front door when the first shot rang out.

I fell flat to the sidewalk. I didn't typically carry a gun and now wasn't one of those rare occasions where I did. It certainly would have been better if I had.

Burke, on the other hand, had pulled out a four-inch .38 Special revolver with a deep grained wood handle. The big man worked quickly on his feet. He shifted from left to right and back again. When the second shot came, he got a fix on the shooter and shot back. I witnessed pure textbook firearms usage, right out of the police academy, although Burke would never have gained access.

Rather than stay stagnant and become a target, he moved about ten feet forward, slightly off to his left side and stood just in the middle of the street. He fired twice.

The shooter was across the way in the Howse Public Parking. He moved out from behind a pillar and tried to gain access to the sidewalk and round the corner onto East William. He practically tripped over his own shoes.

Burke's third shot hit the shooter in the upper thigh. A yelp filled the air. As he started to go down, Burke's fourth shot caught the guy's chest. The guy flew off his feet backward and landed with a thud. It sounded like his head cracked against the pavement.

I got up, and we ran across the street. I recognized the shabby suit before Burke had even turned him over. It was Mickey Dowell. Blood gushed from his thigh and out of his chest with each diminishing breath. Before I could even think to ask him anything he was dead.

Burke holstered his weapon and turned to me with a kind of paternal pride.

"I think you owe me a couple of drinks for saving your life," he said smugly.

"How do we know he wasn't aiming for you?"

Burke shrugged. He didn't need to admit to the possibility. The threat ended when the man died. All that remained was the anticipated bureaucracy.

Police headquarters was a mere four blocks away. The shots resulted in a phone call from someone at the Flanagan Mortuary who prepared for a service within the hour. Max Burke and I settled into the building I had spent four years in. He didn't seem as comfortable as me.

Bill Ward of the Night Detective Squad had just come on duty. Clarence Mendenhall would be on in about another hour or so. Max Burke's story of a private detective working on a missing person's case that happened to coincide with my case sounded reasonable enough. After a mutual agreement to share information, the deceased fired upon us. Bill asked Burke to repeat himself a few times. He didn't really ask me much. Either he figured I had an angle to play and would get around to fill him and Mendenhall in on it later.

I let Burke run with it. At this point, it made no sense to spill the beans given how little I knew or understood about the situation. On top of that, I wasn't just slapping back at Burke by the suggestion he could have just as easily been the target. After all, Burke had Mickey try to convince me to play ball. Burke seemed frightened by the knowledge Dowell was looking for him. That put the ball in Burke's court.

Then again, Mickey Dowell lived hand to mouth and took on anything that would give him bread and booze money. After his termination from the police department, he didn't have any scruples to differentiate between the good guys and the bad. Who knows? Maybe he never did. Whatever he was up to at that moment, he didn't seem beholden to Max Burke.

They cut us loose just after nine o'clock. I reiterated my offer of a drink or two. I knew Burke would accept.

The Surf Lounge had an ironic name for a joint in a state that didn't have palm trees, white sand beaches, or even blue water. Probably the type of place you would find all over Sunset Strip. For a short spell, the darkness kept us far removed from College Hill, Plainview, or the police station.

"Come on. Give," I said after the waitress brought two drinks to our booth.

"What?"

I gave him a stare to show I was tired and fed up.

"What's the frammis? This isn't about stag pictures. What are you onto?"

He leaned in close. Even with no one on either side of us, he had the need for more privacy. A bit of fear started to seep into his beady eyes.

"Brooks Mellon was like your dead pal, Mickey Dowell. Only he hung around with a better class of people."

"Such as?"

"I'll give you two names. Jack Dragna and Robert G. Thompson."

The police considered Dragna the Capone of Los Angeles, a powerful mob boss who dealt with the East Coast contingent represented by Bugsy Siegel and Meyer Lansky, a couple of Jews I would not consider associating with. Thompson was a name I only vaguely knew. Burke described him as a decorated soldier who now headed up the New York branch of the Communist Party of America.

"What was Mellon's involvement with either of them?"

Burke shrugged his shoulders.

"But I guarantee you one thing," he said, "it didn't have to do with stag films. Brooks was about money. He would do whatever he could to put a bankroll in his pocket. Loved good food, good booze, and cheap broads."

"How does Debra Rose Nathan fit into this?"

"The way I figure is she stumbled across Brooks after he had been killed and grabbed something that someone thought might have been important and worth some dough."

"So, you shlep on out here on a hunch, come across me, and try to get me to do your dirty work for you?"

"Listen, chum. I'm in this for a payout. You're looking for a girl. It's the same thing. You get it?"

I reached over and grabbed his wrist. I made it out to be a gesture of control because I grew tired of relinquishing it so often.

"Now, you listen, chum. We have no idea who Mickey Dowell was gunning for. Could have been both of us, especially if what you're suggesting is true. Since you've come into my life, I've encountered a guy who lost an election but still acts like a politician, an art aficionado who suggested I keep my nose out of an unnamed business that involved your buddy Brooks, a remarkably strange gallery curator who seems to have no idea what is going on, and a thug that would burst your bubble without batting an eyelash. You don't have nearly enough muscle or bullets to fight your way out of whatever this is. You're in over your head and dragging me down with you."

He wrenched his arm away from my grip.

"That is why I'm telling you we've got to work together. All right, I'm out of my element here. I don't know Midwest folks. You do. You didn't even pull out a gun. What kind of soldier were you anyway?"

That kind of comment got to me more than those about my religion. I gave up the dreams of a career as a detective sergeant to serve my country and defend it from a greater evil. I might not have been as selfless as Dick Cowan, but I fought without fear until I could fight no more. I knew that giving in to such rhetoric would only cloud my thinking.

I had to admit Max Burke and I fit together for this task. But just for this task. I didn't need another drink to convince me of that. Yet I still had a feeling in the pit of my stomach that he fed me only an hors d'oeuvre and the main course was still to come.

He would reach out to his contacts in Los Angeles to follow up on Brooks Mellon's murder. I didn't let him know I had been in touch with Detective Noone. I figured I would compare the official reports to whatever he found and see what he might have left out. In the meantime, I would backtrack on Mickey Dowell. A guy like him wasn't too keen about covering his tracks. I still knew a few folks from his part of town that would bend under the weight of a dollar bill.

Maybe it would have been smart to bring Max with me if I tried to brace Zach Molloy. Then again, I didn't think there was much chance to get that block of concrete to divulge anything more than snappy patter and a desire to cause someone pain. He didn't scare, wasn't moved by threats, or cracked under pressure. Like Mount Etna, his explosion would come in due time.

It started to get late, and it had already been a long day. I told Burke to meet me at the Carnegie Library on Monday at ten in the morning. It would be interesting to get Carla Duggan's take on this guy as well as see if she couldn't cut him down to size.

For now, I needed to let him go his own way and hope he wouldn't try to grab the brass ring by himself. I had done all I could to convince him I was only after the girl and not the pot of gold at the end of the rainbow. Deep down, I didn't think it would amount to much. Then again, I was prepared to be wrong.

Chapter Nineteen

It was necessary to have some quiet time on Sunday morning. Me and the cats and a decent breakfast. I fried two eggs, had some toast and fresh squeezed orange juice, and brewed a full pot of coffee. As I grabbed the Beacon from outside my front door, Ralph and Marion Skelton were on their way to church.

"More exciting adventures, Mr. Bergman?" Mrs. Skelton asked with a bit of a giggle in her voice.

"Believe me, you don't want to know."

No one would mistake me for Bob Hope, but I could not be more serious. If my quaint and sedate neighbors truly knew what kind of people I encountered in my line of work, they would likely never leave their apartments. Sometimes I didn't want to as well, but it made no sense to hide from the darkness when I was able to carry the light.

I divided a can of Strongheart cat food between Lady Mittens and Sir Pounce. It only made sense that we should all have a good breakfast. Although I didn't appreciate the notion the label identified it as for both dogs and cats. Their quiet feeding frenzy indicated they didn't seem to mind. Although they might take umbrage should a canine intrude on their repast.

After I cleaned the dishes, I took out a note pad and made a list. I needed to get organized given that I had almost too much information with none of it leading anywhere. It turned into a lot of noise as opposed to a well-planned symphony.

On the Martin Kaye death, I had a wife who initially claimed her husband didn't drink but a coroner's report that indicated a near overdose of paraldehyde, a drug known to curb and possibly cure alcoholics. The main person who considered his death murder was himself an alcoholic former attorney who worked as a clerk in an insurance firm who desperately wanted the death to be suicide. A clinic in town advised Kaye demanded only a prescription for the paraldehyde much to their chagrin. There were enough clients who may have been bilked which gave me a larger than usual suspect pool. Finally, I had Sharon Kaye, who, for my money, was a conniving schemer, even though she was my client.

Given both the initial and the follow-up report from the coroner, I had a hard time envisioning the kind of murder caused by emotional duress. The blunt force trauma turned out to be so minimal as to be an oversight. A disgruntled client would pick up a rock or a paperweight and bring it crashing down on Kaye's head. This was more of a bump or a bruise.

Murder by poison, more specifically an overdose of paraldehyde, had likelier possibilities. The question was how it was introduced.

The guys at the insurance firm knew more than they admitted to. I would need to meet with Kelly Gardner, the clerk, in front of his employers if I were to light a fire under them and get some definitive answers. I wrote down a note to go to their office late Monday morning after I met with Burke at the library.

Debra Rose Nathan was invisible for all I knew. Her stay in Los Angeles spooked her enough to rush back home to Kansas where in a matter of days she just up and vanished. I firmly believed she had not simply gone off somewhere else to follow a dream. What other dream could there be? But for the life of me I just couldn't figure out what she had taken or brought back with her from the West Coast that would have made so many people's heads spin.

Stag photos were not important enough. Industrial plans, a bald-faced lie. Photos of valuable art purchased for a song fell into the same category. Perhaps she took nothing, only someone presumed she had. An invisible girl with an invisible item of value.

Lady Mittens jumped up on my lap and momentarily forced me to put my pencil down. I playfully scratched her ear. Sir Pounce jumped on the table and aroused my gentle ire which sent the dear girl off my lap. The moment of peace vanished.

I sat in my favorite chair in the parlor and read from the Talmud when I came across a passage that seemed to resonate: "If you lift the load with me, I will be able to lift it; and you will not, I won't lift it." While I respected the sentiment, I understood how my profession, this journey I had willfully accepted as my own, was about finding strength in the middle of hopelessness. I couldn't give up because of integrity and obligation.

Perhaps in one regard I relived my experiences from the war. They trained us that our squad, our platoon, our company, and so on were the backbone of the military. These groups of men were brothers in arms. Regardless of background or intelligence or religion, we had a collective strength. They instilled this sensibility in us for the sole purpose of keeping fear at bay.

In this world of city streets and back alleys and

wealthy homes, I needed to rely on my education even before the army. My upbringing, the house of my parents, my religion, the One we prayed to in temple. So, perhaps that phrase meant I should seek more help from God. Max Burke was a poor substitute.

I needed some fresh air to clear my head of the clouds I created. At this point, the well-satiated cats slept soundly on my bed and didn't require my complete attention. I started to walk in the general vicinity of downtown and thought about grabbing another cup of coffee at King's X. It would also be prudent to see if Jennie Palmer had any youthful words of wisdom for me.

A black sedan, one I had seen before, passed me as I walked south on Market Street, made a loud U turn, and then pulled up alongside me. It was Ralph Dewald who looked cheerful and chipper but for what reason I couldn't say.

"Hey, there, Bergman."

I stepped off the curb and leaned in through the passenger window.

"Good morning, Mr. Dewald."

"You know, I had planned to stop by and visit you after noon, you know, when church got out. Then I remembered you don't go to church on account of you being Jewish."

He seemed rather pleased with his intelligence. It had no impact on me.

"What can I do for you?" I wasn't cold or blunt but neither friendly nor welcoming either. I guess you could say I became bored in anticipation of more lies, yet at the same time eager to hear them, if not for information than for entertainment.

"Can I buy you a cup of coffee, Mr. Bergman?"

"I was just heading down to the King's X."

He leaned over, opened the door, and I hopped in.

We sat at the counter. I always figured guys like Dewald wanted to keep their interactions in secret, keep their voices down, hide their mannerisms, as though any word or gesture might be a clue they didn't want someone to hear or see. Too many people lived their lives in secrecy. That was part of the problem with the world today.

"Personally, I think Alan was a little rough on you the other night." I gave him a blank stare. "Alan Isbell." I nodded, almost yawning. "You're just a guy trying to earn a living, make an honest dollar. Am I right?"

"Absolutely."

I watched him take the sugar dispenser and hold it upside down. It looked like an hourglass as time ticked away.

"Well, I told him that it would probably be better if we just let you go about your business and offer you a finder's fee if you were successful."

I turned on my stool, my elbow on the counter, my hand holding my head up.

"What is it you people think I'm looking for?"

For whatever reason, I caught him off guard. It was as though he had prepared a stump speech that he prepared to bull his way through, but I interrupted with a meaningful question, one he didn't anticipate.

"Well, the girl, of course."

"And you'll give me a finder's fee. If I find her."

He smiled as he stifled back a laugh. I had no idea what kind of joke I had just told. I guess I was funnier than I thought.

"Look, we know Arlene Nathan doesn't have a pot

to pee in and that jazz musician is her only friend in the world. How are they going to pay your fee?"

His comment hadn't been meant as rude or dismissive. In his mind, he simply stated facts as he saw them. People like him only considered facts and almost always forgot about people.

"Do you know what *tzedakah* is, Mr. Dewald?"

"No."

"Technically it means 'righteousness'; however, in common usage it refers to charity. Not just simple giving but the kind born from moral obligation. So, if it is within my heart to do this work for Mrs. Nathan without monetary compensation, it is I who will be blessed. You see, folks like you and Alan Isbell see the world in terms of possessions, what you can buy and sell. And this extends to people."

"You can spare me your highfalutin platitudes, Mr. Bergman. All we were trying to do is ensure you get paid for your services."

"You've said 'we' a few times, Mr. Dewald. Who are you referring to?"

"The Hephaestus Society."

"Would you mind explaining what interest an arts group has in hydroelectric generators?"

"What?"

"Well, that's what you told me this was about several nights ago. Didn't you?"

He stood up gruffly, pulled a couple of dollars out of his pocket, and threw them on the counter. It didn't appear he planned to offer me a ride home.

"We'll be in touch."

"I'll be breathlessly waiting. For all of you."

He stormed off, slammed his car door, and drove off

like Wilbur Shaw. After dealing with Albert Whitman, I had a bad taste in my mouth for affluent men who seemed unconnected to the real world. Perhaps I was naïve to think foot soldiers meant anything on the pavement. The generals, in this case men like Alan Isbell, ran the whole operation without the rest of us even aware.

Jennie Palmer came over and refreshed my coffee. She had a questioning smirk on her face but knew better than to inquire more deeply. She did, however, lean in with some friendly advice.

"There has been a car parked across the way for a good long time, shortly before you got here. Driver hasn't gotten out or moved. Except when that fella left and took off."

"Could be anybody," I replied.

"Could be," she responded with a knowing smile.

While the rest of me remained calm, my foot started to throb a bit from the excitement. I wondered whether the walk home would relax it or exacerbate it. There was only one way to tell.

A gray two-door Nash parked on the southeast corner of First Street and Broadway. I thought I had seen it when I came out of my apartment earlier. When Dewald first accosted me, I noticed it drive past us pretty quickly. I tried to remember where I had seen it before. I started to walk home.

Since First went one way east, I turned back west toward Market Street. I knew the car would have to make some moves if it were truly following me. Then again, it might figure I headed home. Since my residence hadn't been a secret to anyone, there was just as much of a chance I would find it parked out front.

Just as I started to cross Second Street, which headed one way west, the Nash drove past me. This wasn't my imagination. I saw nothing further until I got to the First Presbyterian Church. The front of the church faced Broadway; the Nash sat idly in their back parking lot. This car started to rattle me. I felt torn between uncertainty and anger. I had half a mind to walk straight up to it and confront the driver, but my ankle throbbed. A faster walk was not on the bill at this time. Two more blocks and I'd be home. I didn't make it.

As I walked north on the east side of the street, I heard the Nash race out from where it was, past me, and into the parking lot of the Commodore Apartments on the southeast corner of Market and Elm. The car turned in such a fashion that the driver's side faced me as I approached.

The window rolled down quickly. In that instant, I remembered I saw the car at Alan Isbell's house. It was Dorothy Martin.

"We need to talk." She didn't look like the curator of an art gallery.

Chapter Twenty

She said we needed to talk, someplace in private. I suggested my apartment. She said everyone knew where I lived. After all, I had an ad in the Polk directory. Then she added we should also avoid the Pan American Café as everyone knew of my friendship with King Mar. That might be common knowledge in and around Wichita, but I had no idea how someone from Pennsylvania would reference it. What I didn't know could fill an encyclopedia.

I thought of Nicholas Leonides, my Greek friend who ran a small food mart on the corner of Douglas and Topeka. They offered traditional specialties along with basic items. He also had a couple of spare rooms at the top of his store that he offered on occasion to those in a particular kind of need. Alonzo Washington learned of Leonides' hospitality before. Late Sunday afternoon before closing time suited our needs.

I stepped in the front door, made eye contact with Nicholas' son Gilbert, and then went around back where a staircase led to the upper floor. It was funny how those stairs reminded me in one regard of Jacob's ladder.

Dorothy Martin followed stealthily while she looked back over her shoulder in a manner that indicated similar training to what I had at the police academy. Gallery curators typically didn't act that way.

As we got into the hallway where doors on either

side led to each room, Nicholas himself greeted me. He had a more paternal look of concern than anything else. He knew better than to ask.

"Fifteen minutes," I said. "Thirty tops, Nick."

"No worries. We're closing shop soon. No one will hear you."

He made no direct eye contact with Miss Martin. While I knew part of his background, his actions over the years led me to realize I didn't know the whole story. As a friend, I never asked for details. It was more compelling to imagine.

I closed the door and sat on a chair at the desk, more for the comfort of my foot than any social propriety. Miss Martin stood before me and acted somewhere between a teacher and a prison guard. From inside her jacket, she pulled out what at first looked like a billfold. They were, in fact, credentials: Federal Bureau of Investigation.

"I don't know what case you're currently working on, Mr. Bergman, but you have inadvertently stepped into a matter of extreme national security." Her tone came out clipped and precise. I often wondered if agents took classes in how to handle private citizens.

"I'm looking for a missing girl."

"Regrettably, that pales in comparison to our current investigation."

"I don't think so." I caught her off guard with my abrupt directness. She likely imagined her assumed superiority awed other people. "I fought for my country."

"We are aware of that."

"I fought for people like Arlene Nathan," I continued. "Mothers, fathers, sons, and daughters. Whatever it is that is threatening national security shouldn't require basic folks to make those kinds of sacrifices."

She quietly exhaled. She figured this would be a simple castigating lecture filled with highly relevant patriotic intentions that I would simply stand down and thank her for protecting me. While "they" may have known where I lived and where I ate, they would never be able to look into my heart or soul. I knew of no training for that.

"This is highly confidential information I am about to provide. We are trusting your status as a veteran and professionalism in law enforcement to maintain your discretion." I nodded affirmatively. "Brooks Mellon had graduated from cheap stag photos and petty larceny into the world of espionage. We can't say for sure if he embraced the ideals of those involved or if he was in it for the money. My guess is the latter given his lifestyle. His studio was what you would call a way station for passing information. Microfilm or other documents would be brought to him and then picked up by another courier. Often this would be a matter of hours. At times, no more than a day."

"If you knew all of this, why didn't you arrest him?"

"As you can imagine, he was a nothing. A two-bit penny-ante punk who had no idea what kind of information passed through his hands. His loss to whatever organization he was involved with would be of little consequence. No, we wanted the bigwigs. We needed them. The Brooks Mellons of the world are a dime a dozen."

She came across as tough but sanctimonious. I'm sure Hoover loved her.

"And Debra Rose Nathan?"

"We think she grabbed some film she thought were her nudie photos but were likely of greater importance."

"Anything to do with hydroelectric generators?"

She let out a disgusted laugh and sat on the edge of the bed.

"These people have got you on a carousel, Mr. Bergman, and they're spinning you around. No, this has nothing to do with industrial espionage, although Ralph Dewald might have been led to believe that himself. Outside elements have used him for leverage given his propensity for graft."

"Max Burke?"

"A cheap grifter who pretends to be a legitimate PI like you."

"Alan Isbell?"

"Bingo. A man of wealth acquired from undetermined sources even we can't locate, hiding among the recherché of the art world. When you don't know what a man does or how he gets his money, chances are he isn't a priest. Or a rabbi."

I wasn't sure if she said that for my benefit, but it didn't matter. I could appreciate the issue at hand, but I didn't intend to simply go back to Arlene Nathan and tell her national security took more precedence than her daughter. Alan Isbell suggested I step back and now the FBI, in the person of Dorothy Martin, did the same. That gave me even more reason to continue.

"What is your job in all this?" I asked unsure if she would or could answer or if she trusted me enough. Her response surprised me.

"Get close to Isbell and learn what I can. We've got agents stashed around town to back me up if I need to make a play."

"Who?"

She smiled and shook her head. "I'm afraid that is one answer you won't get. Their safety would be in jeopardy if it ever got out."

I had no time for reflection or contemplation. She might have had several plusses in her favor, but I couldn't stop thinking of one poor lonely girl who did nothing more than dream.

"I'm going to continue looking for Debra Rose Nathan," I said defiantly.

"Please do so."

"What?"

"If you wind up getting the lion's share of attention from Alan Isbell and his associates, it'll make it much easier for me to continue my investigation without overt suspicion."

"So, I'm the fox," I said in reference to the British sport.

She stood up, walked over to the door, and put her hand on the knob.

"Good luck, Mr. Bergman," she said over her shoulder before she left. I took that for the answer.

Moments later, Nicholas came in. I heard him but didn't see him. My mind wandered, landing finally on Psalm 72:4: "*He shall judge the poor of the people, he shall save the children of the needy, and shall break in pieces the oppressor.*"

There were too many entities caught in their own perverted thinking. People from some unknown faction who committed espionage hunted by a group we should have called the Good Guys, who themselves tended to overlook basic decency in the name of security. My thoughts ran only to Arlene Nathan and her daughter. It was as simple as that.

I thanked Nicholas again for his hospitality and went back out to Douglas. I found myself further away from home now than before this encounter, and my foot throbbed from stress as much as anything else. A nearby hack brought me home.

Just as I entered the front door, Mrs. Hanover came toward me.

"Could I come in for a moment?"

"Yes, ma'am."

It approached a year of my occupancy there. A passing thought in my mind was she might wish to discuss an increase in the rent. For the second time this afternoon, a woman's response caught me off guard.

"I've been surveying the tenants. None of them were concerned about you taking up one of the three spaces in the back of the building on a permanent basis for your car."

"That is very gracious, Mrs. Hanover, but I don't think it is necessary."

"Well, I have noticed your limp is a bit more pronounced. I used to think that was just because of the cold. But here we are in June. I just think it would help you with your work if you didn't have to walk so much."

It was a touching gesture, one which I acquiesced to in consideration of her commentary. Perhaps I didn't pay attention to my physical limitations quite as much since I did not consider them to be so. Over the course of time, I would run the risk of incapacitating myself by simply not paying attention. In the meantime, I had Mrs. Hanover to watch over me.

A car and a parking spot. Pretty soon, I guessed I would reach out to AT&T to have a phone installed.

Perhaps this investigation service would become more of a business than I realized.

Without knowing why, I looked out my front window which faced Market Street. I glanced from south to north and back again. I didn't know what I looked for and likely wouldn't know it if I saw it. I felt a presence more than saw one.

Mysteries are insignificant if you are not aware of them. Once someone affirms there is a creature in the shadows, one's expectations increase. Dorothy Martin only two days ago presented herself as a vaguely interesting art gallery curator from Pennsylvania. Now she was an FBI agent. Alan Isbell, much like Albert Whitman, came across as a man of wealth who dabbled in all sorts of businesses. As of now, the Feds labelled him as the likely ringmaster of a spy network.

What little I knew of Ralph Dewald gave me to believe he had more interest in the prestige of power or at least being associated with those in power. My intuition suggested he knew little about the inner workings of this group who merely used him for his connections in the city.

However, Max Burke intrigued me because I could no longer be certain of his stake in this game. He came across as fumbling until, that is, he gunned down Mickey Dowell with a proficiency I never expected. He referenced Mellon's connections to gangsters and Communists in a kind of offhanded manner as though he attempted to lead me in a direction he wanted me to go.

At this point, I knew everyone fairly well and could guess what cards they held. Burke was the wild card right now. He seemed to be on my side. As of tomorrow, we would see how close or far apart we were.

Chapter Twenty-one

I figured this to be a busy day. Regrettably, I was already tired from the start of it.

The cats barely opened their eyes when I popped out of bed. They stretched, gave me a disinterested look, and went back to sleep. Each of us had their own schedule. Theirs did not include getting up this early.

I brewed a full pot of coffee and made some oatmeal while I pulled out my notebook to assess each situation, each case on its own merits. Contrary to popular belief as established by Hollywood, private detectives did not simply work in the wee small hours of the morning or the dark recesses of the night. We didn't automatically commiserate with gangsters or criminals. I had no cheap bottle of rye in a desk drawer and plenty of books of matches for the numerous cigarettes I supposedly smoked. I didn't even have a desk with drawers. However, as per my military training, I discovered the early bird does catch the worm. The general public would be surprised by the truth.

Farmers and Bankers Insurance opened promptly at eight in the morning. I got there at seven thirty, sat in my car across the street, and waited like Assault in the starting gate at Churchill Downs. The coffee coursed through me. I needed only to listen for the bell to go off or the whistle to blow.

The ever-efficient Troy Harding arrived at a quarter

till eight and casually unlocked the front door, oblivious to anything else at that hour. He likely did not expect anyone other than Miss Moyer at that hour. Certainly not a fast-approaching nemesis. It appeared he may have gasped as I walked briskly toward the entrance. That might have been my imagination for all I knew. We almost collided as I entered.

"I'm here to see Kelly Gardner. When does he get in?" I asked bluntly.

"Please come back to my office," he responded softly, almost meekly. With his head lowered in defeat, he walked gingerly, like a diplomat who tried to bring the war to an end without firing so much as a volley.

I followed him briskly. He closed the door behind me and then elegantly waved his hand toward a seat in front of his desk. I ignored the gesture, standing at attention like the good soldier I had been. He, however, fell into his seat and then nervously called "Tom" in the office intercom. Within about fifteen seconds, Mr. Van Sickle had joined us. It felt considerably longer. Van Sickle looked like a deflated balloon. Maybe he just didn't have enough coffee.

"When does Kelly Gardner get in?" I repeated.

"Mr. Gardner is no longer employed here." Troy was direct and efficient.

"He was terminated due to ethics violations." Tom Van Sickle was a little more understated. I looked back and forth between Troy and Tom, as though we were old buddies who shared a joke. Like rundown boxers, they waited for the next punch. I started with a jab.

"Well, it seems you have an open position for a freelance investigator. I've got great credentials. Suppose we start with the Kaye life insurance policy."

"Mr. Bergman, won't you have a seat?"

I acquiesced, largely because Troy Harding looked like he might start to cry. The front door opening and closing announced the arrival of Miss Moyer. Someone gasped, but I couldn't tell who.

"Please understand we did appreciate Mr. Gardner's abilities," Van Sickle began. He had the demeanor of a couple of professors I had at Wichita University. A pleasantness meandered in his voice that was both positive and reassuring, yet waiting for an adversarial response. I reminded myself this was a business, not a place of higher learning. "Despite his disbarment, he still had a great value to us. Perhaps we did insinuate the possibility of progressing from a mere research assistant to a position, oh, shall we say, more prestigious. But we never assigned him any specific file to work on and made it perfectly clear the parameters of his position."

"What drew him to the Kaye policy?"

The two of them looked at each other. They tried to decide who would speak next.

"He made a comment to the effect of recognizing Sharon and Martin Kaye but not by those names," Harding responded.

"When did he make the comment?"

"Right after they bought the policy from us," Van Sickle interjected.

"So, he knows something or thinks he knows something that you don't and tries to shake them down?"

"There is that likelihood," Van Sickle responded with a degree of embarrassment.

"Did he quit?"

"We could not allow the possibility an employee would extort a client of ours. It is against every ethical principle of this firm." Troy Harding came across as the epitome of the professionalism of a snake oil salesman.

I sat and thought about it for a moment. Most of it made sense. If any of it were true, the pathetic drunk Gardner had become would be putting himself in harm's way. On the other hand, if his memory failed, he would just sink deeper into oblivion.

"Where does it stand now in terms of paying out?"

"The report of a heavy amount of paraldehyde in Mr. Kaye's system puts the policy in a precarious balance," Harding explained. "It could be accidental. It could just as easily be intentional."

"Murder?"

Troy looked at the blotter on his desk. Tom gazed over my shoulder. They knew that I knew the answer. Withholding it made no sense.

"Perhaps."

"Thank you, gentlemen."

I got up and headed for the door, then stopped to turn around.

"Did Gardner have a drinking problem you were aware of?"

The men looked at each other conspiratorially.

"He had it under control," Harding replied matter-of-factly.

"Until recently," Van Sickle chimed in.

"What was he taking for it?"

A sick gray silence out of a Gothic novel hung over us.

Van Sickle said, "Paraldehyde."

Back in my car, I considered Kelly Gardner simply as a wayward leaf in the wind. He did not have a direct connection with the Kayes, unless, of course, he truly recognized them as someone else. But from where? And what, if any, was his connection to them? Carla Duggan speculated on this during her initial research, but Sharon Kaye casually denied it.

The thought of playing two sides against the middle fell like a rock in the pit of my stomach. Sharon Kaye was, after all, my client. Until I found definitive proof of false testimony or fabricated situations, I had to give her the full and complete benefit of the doubt. By the same token, I needed to ensure I had another iron in the fire in case this fell through.

There were few places around like the Red Apple Filling Station. Up on the thirty-four hundred block of North Broadway, the main building was shaped like, well, a red apple. The Conoco filling station stood beside it. It was a combination grocery store and restaurant. I had never availed myself of either. Until recently no car to need gas and too far out of my area to consider it as a breakfast haunt. That didn't matter much now. At this hour of the day was where one could find Tyler Schenkel.

We didn't go to basic training together nor did we serve together. I met him only on a troop ship that came back from Europe. Two kids from Kansas who had seen enough to last a lifetime. He grew up on a farm down about Mulvane. He was one of those squeaky-clean types who became sullied by the darkness he encountered in battle. We talked on that transport, and I got the impression he wasn't thrilled about a return to a life of tilling and hoeing. The old "Once they've seen Paris" story.

A few months after we got back when I just started in my new career, I ran into him once again. He had the look of a Chicago card sharp or a New York racketeer. I never got a handle on what game he played, but the word was he could get what you needed. That meant anything. To have evolved that quickly merited both fear and respect. Likely that was all he wanted out of life anymore.

He sat at the counter and poured syrup on his flapjacks after every bite, alternating with sips of coffee. His plate a veritable lake of sugary goo. He did not look like a hummingbird. He caught me out of the corner of his eye but continued to eat voraciously.

"Hope I'm not interrupting anything." I was polite but caught myself sounding like Joe E. Brown.

"But you are," he responded, then poured more syrup.

He had a need to assert his importance even though I dismissed it long ago. Nevertheless, I accepted his ribbing.

"What do you hear about Reds in Kansas?"

"You mean injuns?"

"Communists."

He put his fork down, wiped his mouth, finished his coffee, and then threw a couple of dollar bills on the counter before he got up and walked out without another word. I took that as my cue.

We stood several feet from the gas pumps. Cars still moved north and south on Broadway. It wasn't so loud I couldn't hear Tyler through a muffled voice.

"Scuttlebutt is someone is looking for film. Some kind of microfilm. You get me?"

"What's on it?"

"Don't know a thing about it. But the word is they're offering big bucks for it."

"And how does this relate to Reds?"

"That same scuttlebutt is saying Uncle Sam would pay more for it than the someone who is looking for it."

"You got a line on it?"

"No." He turned and looked directly at me with a touch of greed in his eyes. "Do you?"

"Thanks, Tyler."

I couldn't get to my car fast enough. When I was around him, it felt like getting gassed in the trenches. It stuck to you and made you sick. He gave me the thread. The rest I would need to get for myself.

I drove south on Broadway, jogged over to Main Street at Thirteenth, and continued south to the Wichita Carnegie Library. Main Street north of Thirteenth became Park Place. I could have turned earlier and stopped at Bradley and Svetlana's house, but I had an appointment. A quick visit with them would extend to well into the middle of the afternoon. Time became increasingly important as it grew shorter.

To my surprise, Max Burke was more than prompt. Carla had apparently figured out he waited for me and engaged him in conversation. She probably wanted to get a handle on him because, well, that was what she did. And I didn't even need to ask.

"The articles on the Hephaestus Society could have been written by a publicity agent," she started. "They are all glowing with praise in terms of what they do for the artists in Wichita and segments of Sedgwick County. Bravo for them."

"Bradley says they're scoundrels."

"Well, the only identifiable member is Alan Isbell."

"Do you have the scoop on him?"

"Degree in Business Administration from

University of Kansas. Second in his class at Baylor Law School. Passed the bar in Kansas. Accredited for the past twenty-one years."

"What kind of practice does he have?"

"He doesn't," she responded bluntly.

Max and I looked at each other. He didn't know Carla as well as I did. To me, this sounded like a very bad punch line to a silly joke.

"A lawyer without a practice. How does the man afford a home like his in College Hill?"

She shrugged.

"This guy ain't right." Max really did not impress me by his grasp of the obvious. I had to give him the opportunity to show his aptitude for detective work.

"So, what is his connection to a thug like Zach Molloy and a scam artist like Ralph Dewald? There is nothing arts-related about them. At all."

"Mr. Burke might be able to shed some light on that." She sounded entirely too gracious to refer to him in so gentlemanly a fashion. She probably recognized he was a necessary component to this case for the moment.

"Brooks sent me on an errand one afternoon. It had to do with determining if we could shake down a producer over one of his starlets caught on film with reefer. Anyway, as I was returning, a guy was just leaving. I didn't get a good glimpse of him. But Brooks got all excited for some reason."

"Did he tell you why?" I asked.

"Only that a package arrived that he would sell. Could possibly bring in ten grand. He stalled on more info. Kind of alluded to taking care of me, but I knew better than to think Brooks would shell out anything more than a C-note. When he left, I checked out his appointment book. Simply said 'R Dewald' for that day and about the time I left."

"Well, that seems to tie the Los Angeles angle in to Wichita. The question is what was the package? You've got to find out, Burke."

"How?" he said incredulously.

"Do whatever it is you do. Make phone calls. Send telegrams. Something. Anything."

I stormed out when various patrons shushed me after I raised my voice. Burke's quaint comments, unrefined speculations, occasional recollections, and suppositions did not help. Yet, I couldn't deny his marksmanship and was at least grateful for that. However, I needed more.

At this point, I had to determine if my client, Sharon Kaye, would be as forthcoming as her insurance company. Her case ran into the thirteenth day, and a vast uncertainty remained as to whether I could provide proof to her to file the claim.

She dressed in slacks and a short-sleeved shirt. Her leather sandals gave more of an impression of beach attire, rather ironic for Kansas. Wherever she was truly from, surf and sand were more comfortable to her. I noticed a lightness to her step, her mood, and her voice. She was pleased to see me and let me know.

"Believe me, I completely appreciate your dogged efforts regarding my case. It is quite refreshing."

"I base it on both professional and personal ethics."

"I'm sad to say my late husband did not share the same degree of moral strength you possess. I don't know many men who do anymore."

She had me on the verge of a Jimmy Stewart "Aw, shucks, ma'am" mode when a violent knock at the door interrupted. As she opened it, Arnold Sims stormed in.

He still wore the tight Windsor knot and starched white shirt. This time he eliminated the vest. In place of that, he held a snub nose revolver with impressive bluing. He waved it in a wild fashion.

"I've had enough, Mrs. Kaye. I want my money. And as you can see, I am prepared to do what is necessary to get it back."

Sims moved toward Sharon Kaye. I stood off to the side. As he stepped forward, I was out of his view. He was so focused on her he practically hadn't noticed me. When his arm flew up in the air, I dove at him. We fell to the floor together. His head bounced on the carpet, but I could still hear a thud. I held his arm by the wrist and shook it several times until the gun fell from it. I got off him and picked up the gun. After all that, he started to cry.

"Call the police."

This time, I didn't have to spend several hours at the station. Detective George Ledbetter took our statements after Sims was taken away in handcuffs. He noticed as I rubbed my ankle and was courteous enough to inquire if I would need medical attention. After everyone had left, the real surprise came.

Sharon Kaye approached me with an envelope. She handed it to me the same way a man offers a woman an engagement ring.

"I hope this will suffice." She hadn't quite batted her eyelashes, but it came close.

"You understand there is no proof Arnold Sims killed your husband."

"No, but his actions certainly lean toward the possibility of it. I'm sure the insurance company will see it my way now."

The check came to seven hundred and fifty dollars, far more than my usual fee but enough more to make it acceptable to end the case. She extended her hand. I kept it professional with a light shake. That hand felt soft like the petals of a petunia. She had the fragrance to match. I tried not to hold onto her gaze too much. This was a Medusa of rare beauty.

When I got out to my car, I looked at the check closely. I had no concern it was good. What made it seem suspect was that it had been dated the previous Friday.

Chapter Twenty-two

I needed to find Kelly Gardner. Then again, I needed to find Debra Rose Nathan. As I knew all along, people, real live people, were the keys to the answers to many mysteries. It gnawed on me that I had so much information in front of me about both cases but couldn't fit any of it into some kind of a discernible equation, all wrapped up in tissue paper with pink ribbons around it. The funny thing was Rabbi Saperstein was losing his sight yet still could find a deeper vision within. Growing old, man's sight worsens, but this allows him to see more. My only recourse at this point. I had to grasp it with all my might.

From a professional standpoint, the Kaye case was closed. She'd paid me off for services rendered, and that should have been the end of it. Unfortunately, my recent history proved I could not leave well enough alone. Arthur Whitman paid me in full, only too well, after he had made amends with his daughter. That didn't ring any truer than Sharon Kaye giving me a check she made out well before the potential assault by Arnold Sims. I could not imagine she planned that in any fashion. After all, why would Sims sacrifice himself that way and for what recompense? Perhaps Sharon Kaye was already prepared to close the case and this event turned out to be merely a fortuitous opportunity, one that fit in with her insurance case quite neatly. My earlier uncertainty about compensation from Farmers and Bankers Insurance evaporated.

I tried Gardner's apartment first. I found it to be as rundown and dingy in daylight as night time. This time, however, I could see it in all its degradation. The sunshine only enhanced the paleness of the surroundings. Peeling wallpaper in the hall and a threadbare runner looked like the last stop of a long journey. The aggressive knocks on the door yielded no response. As I started to leave, an old woman, wrinkled and barely able to stand, spoke out in a loud clear voice.

"You lookin' for Kelly?" I nodded, uncertain of how else to respond. "This time of day, he's likely up at the Royal Lounge."

"Right around the corner on Central?"

"The same."

I had half a thought in my mind to give her two bits, but it wasn't the kind of *tzedakah* she needed. I nodded in gracious thanks, then regretted I didn't do any more.

You couldn't even call the Royal Lounge a dive. It was always dark because they kept the wooden blinds closed regardless of the hour of the day. A long bar ran down one side and three tables with two chairs apiece stood along the windows, lonely and vacant. Perhaps a crack of light entered but for the most part you couldn't see anyone, probably the way the habitués preferred it. The silence and emptiness of darkness was a warm comforting blanket.

Kelly Gardner sat at the end of the bar and sipped from a small shot glass, oblivious to the world beyond his stool. I had no way of telling how many he consumed. From his diminished efforts to hold himself upright, I would have guessed a lot.

When I approached, he patted the seat beside him. He either remembered me or looked for company. In either case, he was rather gregarious.

"I figured you'd find me," he slurred through a thick tongue. "Anyone can. And chances are if you did, she will."

"Sharon Kaye?"

"Yep."

"Why would she be looking for you?"

"She knows."

"Knows what?"

He leaned in close. His breath was foul and almost medicinal. The booze had both an incapacitating and clarifying effect on him, as though it forced him to tell the truth but didn't allow him to do anything about it. It was a state of immobility, both physical and spiritual, like being in Gehenna with a cocktail in hand.

"Her husband paid me for my paraldehyde."

"Why would he do that?"

"His doctor wouldn't give him enough."

I tried to make some sense from the words of a man in the throes of alcoholic hallucinations. I was nowhere near his state and had a hard time figuring it out.

"Why did he need more?"

He turned slowly to face me, mournful eyes on the verge of tears.

"You know what happens when you overdose on it?"

"So, he wanted to commit suicide?"

He shrugged his shoulders and went back to tiny sips of his drink.

"That right there will sink her claim."

For a moment, he spoke with the clarity of a trial

lawyer as he enunciated the nuances of a case. It was a precision that came through his muddled mind as though he still barely held on to the memory of a more successful past.

"Who else knows?"

"Just me," he proclaimed proudly, as he held his shot glass up toward the bartender.

"We've got to get you out of here."

He threw his arm in my direction and shrugged me off.

"No. S'better this way."

The bartender filled the shot glass and looked at me with contempt. As far as he was concerned, I interfered with a paying customer. I had no certainty Sharon Kaye would attempt any harm against Kelly Gardner just as the attack in her apartment would not guarantee a successful resolution to her claim. The fact remained that either could happen. Or neither. Fate lay elsewhere, certainly not in our own hands.

I couldn't convince Gardner to allow me to help him. The only way to do so was to get Sharon Kaye to relinquish the claim and make him a useless factor. I drove back to Farmers and Bankers Insurance prepared to assist them. To my betterment, of course.

Troy Harding did not appear surprised to see me. He waved me into his office quietly and closed the door behind us. He did not call in Thomas Van Sickle.

"The Kaye policy is for twenty-five thousand, correct?" I got a positive nod in response. "Would it be worth five percent to have Sharon Kaye drop the claim?"

He stared at me perplexed. If it were me, I would be uncertain how to respond to such an offer. There were both professional and ethical considerations. I tried to make it easier for him.

"I don't understand," he said, almost like a confused child, although I knew he egged me on for clarification.

"My understanding of this racket is an investigator for an insurance company, especially a freelance one, usually gets a percentage for the recovery of stolen merchandise, for example."

"That, of course, is accurate. But this is a life insurance policy. A man died. There is nothing to actually recover."

"True. But if the cause of his death were proven to violate the terms of the policy, you wouldn't have to pay. In essence, it would be recovery of funds attempted to be stolen."

"And you can prove such a violation?" It almost sounded like a radio quiz show, his voice as velvety as one of those announcers.

"I'm certain I can get Sharon Kaye to sign a waiver."

We stared at each other like Alexander Alekhine and Max Euwe contemplating a Queen sacrifice. The silence proved more uncomfortable for him than me. He opened a drawer and withdrew a form. He slid it across his desk.

"If you were successful at getting Mrs. Kaye to sign this form, we would be glad to pay you three percent of the policy's value."

"Five." I held up my hand, fingers splayed wide in emphasis of my request. "Five percent." He sighed heavily, then nodded. "In writing," I added, my words a sharp dagger.

I left their office with two forms. One was the waiver; the other, a notarized requisition form authorizing five percent of the Kaye's life insurance policy for "services rendered."

It was just after four o'clock when I knocked on Sharon Kaye's apartment door. She dressed in evening wear: a green short-sleeved floral print dress with a deep decolletage that fit tight at the waist and hugged her hips before slimming down at the thighs and ankles. A moderate ruffle finished off the hem. Accompanying this wardrobe was a sparkly necklace that drew attention to her bosom and dangling earrings that glistened. Overall, an outfit completely unbefitting a grieving widow. She had a warm inviting smile, succulent and deadly, the kind a black widow spider might present if it had lips and teeth and tongue.

"Why, Mr. Bergman. This is quite a pleasant surprise."

"I didn't mean to catch you off guard. I hope I'm not keeping you from anything…important."

"My plans are always subject to change. A woman's prerogative they say."

"Good."

The door opened wider. A wide sweeping arm gesture became a grand invitation. Perhaps gladiators in the Coliseum were offered the same welcome, akin to a reminder of life before their imminent death.

"To what do I owe the pleasure?" The dialogue was straight out of a B melodrama. The emphasis came on the last word. I wasn't sure whose she referred to.

"Well, Mrs. Kaye—"

"Sharon. Please." I heard the pleading tone of a woman filled with unrequited passion. Perhaps her late husband's drunkenness prevented any real expressions of desire.

"Okay, Sharon." I stopped suddenly as though I were confused. "Are you sure it isn't Susan? Susan

King? Or Sophia Klingman? Maybe Samantha Kronauer?"

Her smile remained. The joie de vivre behind it had faded. I wondered what her next move would be.

"I believe we had this discussion just a week ago. At that time, you did not doubt my integrity. And now?"

"Now there is no need to doubt your integrity or anything else about you. As Harold Bergman, private investigator, you have paid me in full for my work on your case."

"So, there is nothing further to discuss."

"Not quite. As an investigator in the employ of Farmers and Bankers Insurance, I have a fiduciary responsibility to secure the assets of the company. A few phone calls to the police departments in Greensboro, Charlottesville, and Wilkes-Barre and I'm certain we could get a wire with complete files of those fraud cases. Maybe even a radiofax if any pictures are available. Which, I'm sure, there are. After that, we bring in Horatio Frazier and Reginald Kraft and before you know it a life insurance policy claim against Farmers and Bankers will be the least of your worries."

She applauded slowly, like a teacher pleased with a child's performance.

"A very noble and brave speech. I'm surprised you didn't include any references to Saint Crispin's Day. Well, you and your band of brothers need not worry, Mr. Bergman."

She looked over her shoulder. I followed her gaze to two large suitcases packed full as they sat in the doorway to the bedroom. The melodrama continued.

"He couldn't take it anymore, could he?"

"No. He never really did have the stomach for it, no

matter how much money we stashed away. So, I acquiesced. I told him we would finish up here and head off to Europe. With the war over, we could live exceptionally well. The way I prefer." She did not need to elaborate.

"Where did Kelly Gardner recognize you from?"

"He didn't." That caught me off guard. "He recognized a fellow drunk in Martin. We hadn't seen this Gardner before we went into the insurance agency. And when Martin decided to bow out, as it were, he got what he needed from him."

"Why on earth would you hire me to prove something you knew I couldn't?"

She shrugged her shoulders. It was so blasé and dismissive I couldn't believe this was a discussion about her husband's suicide.

"Nothing more than a long shot. And well worth the money I paid you. Just a gamble. But sometimes the horse you bet on is only a nag."

I presented the waiver to her. She signed it with aplomb, as though she were a celebrity giving an autograph.

"Well, I was going to have one final night on the town. But under the circumstances, I don't feel all that festive. Would you be so kind as to give me a lift to Union Station? I'm just going to change. It won't be but a moment."

"Rather a shame you must. It is really quite an engaging ensemble."

She smiled lasciviously. In the end, we were two professionals at opposite ends of the game who had no chance to meet in the middle. While I despised her past actions, I respected her integrity enough to realize her recompense was not my responsibility.

Within five minutes, she dressed for traveling. Like a dutiful porter, I carried her bags downstairs and put them in the backseat of my car. I even held the door open for her. On the ride, I asked her where she would go. She casually responded she would take the first train out of town she could and start fresh somewhere else. It was just as likely she didn't want me to keep tabs on her and advise the local authorities. If I wanted to, I could have followed up and checked the ticket counter to wire ahead to the police department wherever she headed. As I recalled from Proverbs 26:27, it didn't seem worth it.

As I took her suitcases from my car, I wondered if she might tip me as one would someone who performed such a task. The surprise came in the form of a brief kiss on my cheek before she turned and left for good.

With the signed waiver in my pocket, I drove back to the insurance office and got there just past four thirty. I met with Troy Harding and Thomas Van Sickle. A bit of nervousness exuded from their looks. My efficiency likely perplexed, them. They both took turns to review the document. Each of them commented with a verbal stamp of approval. Harding made a phone call to the bank, his tone insistent, almost demanding, yet completely professional. His smile was polite after the call.

The three of us waited patiently in an uncomfortable silence. There were a few brief references to my skills and discretion. While it wasn't necessarily an offer, a mention of future freelance investigations dangled like a squirming worm on a hook. It might have been financially advantageous to grab the bait, but I decided I did not want to become Joseph in pharaoh's house just yet.

There were apologies as it droned on past five. Just at a quarter after, a man with round glasses and a very worn business suit knocked politely, entered, and handed Troy Harding an envelope. He nodded and left.

I left the offices of Farmers and Bankers Insurance with a certified check for one thousand two hundred and fifty dollars. Being a freelance insurance investigator seemed easy. Heck, they might make a radio program out of me some day.

Chapter Twenty-three

For the second morning in a row, I got up relatively early. This time it was not by my choice. The gentle rapping on the door was far less violent than that of Arnold Sims yesterday at Sharon Kaye's apartment at the Commodore. This was the restrained knock of official inquiry.

Clarence Mendenhall of the Night Detective Squad looked like he had slept in an open grave. He never had much issue with the late hours in the past. I guessed the previous evening stretched the limits of his constitution. I knew too well such was prone to happen for that profession.

"Bill Ward told me about that shooting the other night. You know much about this Max Burke fella?"

"Enough."

"Well, here's an extra for you. He's over at St. Francis Hospital."

"What?"

"Someone tried to plug him. Took one in the shoulder and one in the belly. Fortunately, he has a big enough belly it didn't do much damage. He lost a lot of blood though, but they've apparently given him transfusions."

"Is he gonna live?"

Mendenhall yawned and then rubbed his eyes. He needed to wrap up his visit and head on home.

"They said so."

He just looked at me blankly.

"Tough night?" I asked with knowing empathy.

"We caught a hit and run that just didn't seem kosher to me. No disrespect."

"None taken. What was wrong with it?"

"Up near MacDonald Golf Course over on North Yale."

"Tight curvy little roads. Might be easy to lose control."

"Yeah, but no one typically speeds around there. And then there were no tire marks, so it wasn't like someone slammed on their brakes. The guy wound up pretty well crushed. We figure it to be a big car, maybe a limo."

"Is he a John Doe?"

"Oh, no. You've heard of him. I just hope you didn't vote for him."

"Vote for him? Who was it?"

"Ralph Dewald."

My jaw dropped almost as dramatically as a character in a Disney cartoon. Mendenhall suddenly snapped out of his stupor and tried to shake me out of mine.

"What gives?" he said.

"These two might be tied together. The golf course is less than a mile from—"

My voice dropped off.

"From what?"

"I'll meet you at the police station this time tomorrow morning."

"Bergman, what have you got?"

"If I'm right, it's big."

He acquiesced and headed on home. As intrigued as he was, there wasn't much left in him after the long night and a case that now caused him to turn an accident into a likely murder investigation.

Max Burke rested quietly when I walked in, but then his mood perked up. I didn't imagine for a moment he would be thrilled to see me. His type never wanted to show pain or fear. Too much a sign of weakness. Californians have a bad rap for being too casual. This bird played it tough all the way. He would have been better suited to the East Coast or Chicago.

"If you wanted off this case, you should have just let me know," I joshed.

"Nothing's getting me off this case, brother. I haven't seen a bullet yet that could put me down."

Here he was in a hospital bed. I begged to differ but let it go.

"What happened?"

"I staked out that Isbell guy, got hungry, and left to find one of those King's X joints."

"Nearby."

"Yeah."

"That would have been Douglas and Hillside. Go on."

"I noticed a car had followed me, so I just parked my keister at the counter where I could see out the window and took my time with a burger and a couple of cups of coffee. And by the way, that place has got nothing on Original Tommy's. Their burgers beat them all."

"Would you forget the food review?"

"Well, sure enough a big black Packard drove by one way and then a few minutes later the other way. It wasn't coy, if you know what I mean. My car sat out front so I couldn't ditch him. Figured the best way was to at least drive around in some areas where there were people. Maybe lose him in a crowd."

"So?"

"I wound up driving north and turned straight into a cemetery."

Maple Grove was probably the second oldest cemetery in Wichita, not what you would call an appropriate place for a car chase. There also weren't many places to hide, especially if you were alive.

"How did he get you?"

"Well, I stupidly got out of my car and hunkered down into some kind of stone pavilion. At that point, I got steamed and thought it would be best to draw him out."

"But he shot you."

"Yeah, but I winged him, too."

Burke then said the shooting stopped for about a minute, at which point he jumped back in his car, and drove to the hospital. He made a full report except he gave the police a description of a completely different car. I didn't want to argue with him about whether it was the right thing to do or not because I half believed he was justified. He indicated he planned to discharge himself now that they got him patched up.

"I don't plan on missing the fireworks," he said stoically.

"The fourth of July is two days away. You won't."

"You know that isn't what I mean."

His face turned as sour as curdled milk. He was upset and feeling mean. Perhaps he thought Wichita to be a Podunk town compared to Los Angeles and that getting shot was an unforgiveable degradation. He would need to find a way to get over his disappointment. Finding out who shot him and getting even would be a good start. At this point, I figured he would find me once he left the hospital. The lone wolf would not cut mustard anymore.

As I walked down the hallway, I came across Charlie Argento who came out of another patient's room. Charlie was a cabbie with a wife and two daughters. He always had a need for money in his household. Many times he bent a few laws, but as far as I knew he never broke any.

"Hiya, Charlie."

"Mr. Bergman, how did you know?"

"Know about what?"

"Richie."

Richie Mayer was five or six years younger than me and 4F on account of acute asthma. He drove a hack as well as being my de facto driver on most occasions unless he had an attack. All he could do then was go home and sleep.

"I didn't know anything about Richie."

"Well, you better go in. He'd sure be glad to see you."

From my experiences in the war, talk like this meant someone checked out and wanted to make their farewells. Since the gift of a car from King Mar, I had not really kept up with Richie or Charlie unlike the many months past.

I couldn't help but notice the prevalence of white. The walls, the sheets, the metal stand that hovered over the bed, and even Richie's hospital gown. I suppose it was better than darker and more depressing colors. He stared at the ceiling when I walked in, surprised to see me, but almost self-conscious.

"Hirsch."

"All right. Give," I queried, a smile on my face designed to give some hope.

"Aw, the asthma again. Bad attack. My landlady called an ambulance. Just about embarrassed me."

"Yeah, but think about what would have happened if she hadn't." He didn't respond. "So, what does the doctor say?"

"I ain't getting any better. That's for sure. He recommended the mountains. Says the air's easier to breathe. Fewer attacks."

"Well, that certainly sounds worthwhile."

"I got a cousin up in Boulder, Colorado. He tried a couple of times to get me to move there."

"Driving a hack?"

"Nah, he's got a small brewery. Wants to open a pub. You see me being a bartender?"

I put my hand gently on his arm and gave it a light squeeze.

"I see you doing anything you want, Richie."

We just looked at each other for a moment, the way two brothers would when one went off to college or war, maybe about to get married. I couldn't bear the thought of a goodbye, so I just turned to leave.

"Hey, Hirsch." I turned back around. "Thanks for everything."

I smiled and left before he could see the tears in my eyes.

Maple Grove Cemetery was less than a mile from MacDonald Golf Course and in turn less than a mile from Alan Isbell's home in College Hill. Burke couldn't determine who drove the big Packard or even how many people. It might be a simple matter of getting Mendenhall or even Bill Ward to check on the car's registration. I had visions of Zach Molloy as he gleefully aimed at the heavy-set interloper or while he sadistically rubbed out Dewald after he told the late politician to get out of the car. While it made for a good tale in a Dick Tracy serial, I needed proof. And I would need a valid reason beyond Molloy's penchant for aggressive behavior.

I had no doubt at this point Isbell and the shady Hephaestus Society covered up some other types of criminal plans. How Debra Rose Nathan fit in was undetermined. The fact this much activity went on made me believe the girl was still alive. I had to keep that hope in my head and in my heart.

Molloy had been known to hang out at Droll's English Grill on East Central. It had a lunch counter but also tables with clean white tablecloths. Perhaps the name and ambiance appealed to Molloy's desire for legitimacy and respect. A sledgehammer for a fist accomplished that as well.

I knew he saw me as I entered. A waitress stood just behind him while he ate a steak and baked potato. He tried to eat in a genteel fashion as though this was chateaubriand served at Delmonico's. While his type would fit in with Jack Dragna out in LA, he seemed grossly out of place here.

Fortunately, the waitress hadn't removed the extra chair at the table. It allowed me to comfortably sit next to him. I finally had my turn to play the part of the interloper.

"I don't believe I invited you to lunch," he said in

between delicate bites.

"I just wondered if you had been playing golf lately."

"Dull sport. Plus, you ever see what those guys wear?"

"Memorial Day was a little over a month ago. Anybody you've been paying respects to recently?"

"Nah. None of my friends were saps enough to enlist."

He stopped eating, wiped his mouth, and looked directly at me. I may have been one of those saps, but I certainly wasn't one of his friends.

"What is a nice guy like you doing hanging out with a high-class butter and egg man like Alan Isbell?" My tone was almost that of a rabbi. I just had to laugh at myself.

"Everybody needs a Bruno."

As a muscle for hire, he didn't need to believe in the cause to get paid. His only requirement was to fit in with the crowd. A tuxedo and a posh restaurant would do the trick. It was all nothing more than lipstick on a pig.

"I'm onto you guys."

I knew it to be a risky play on my part. Burke got shot and Ralph Dewald crushed under four giant tires. The people I found myself up against were ruthless. If you smacked, they punched. If you stabbed, they shot. If you injured them, well, they killed you.

"Listen, sheenie, you're not onto anything. You're a bug crawling on my arm. I've got a good mind to swat you."

"You don't have a good mind, Molloy. You're a wind-up toy waiting for your master's voice so you can bark. I'll make it easy for you and Isbell and the

Hephaestus Society. I'm looking for Debra Rose Nathan. Her mother wants her to come back home. Hey, even you had a mother. As far as I know. Think of how she would feel if you went missing. Then again, maybe she dropped you off on someone's doorstep."

"You're pushing it, Bergman."

"I know. And I'm going to push it just far enough to find that girl. Do you hear me? All I'm looking for is the girl. I'm not a cop anymore. I'm private now, and I'm just looking for the girl. Do you understand?"

I couldn't say it enough times, but I needed it to be clear as a bell. He looked at me as his eyes bored a hole in my skull.

He gave me a slight nod. His face started to turn just a little more red. He did everything he could to refrain from losing his temper and trumpet like a stampeding elephant in the zoo. His pride at his ability to maintain a degree of sophistication held him back.

I nodded in return and left.

My entire thought centered around the notion of being up against an even darker and more dangerous adversary than that late Arthur Whitman. I knew I didn't have the physical or financial means to crack this nut. It was all a matter of making it clear I had but the one sole objective. I had to make this dark circle recognize I had no personal stake in their ultimate plans. That was for Dorothy Martin.

Unless young Debra had truly appropriated something she knew about or, heaven forbid, had ingratiated herself into the deadly world of these men, I had a chance to liberate her and lead her toward her salvation. We could leave the rest to the police department and to the Almighty for more divine retribution.

The clouds of some kind of treachery prevented me from the truth. At this point, that didn't matter. I needed to find a scared and troubled girl and bring her back home. That was all.

Chapter Twenty-four

I'd lit the fuse. I had no control over it now. Perhaps it was a mistake to push someone like Zach Molloy. I knew how hard he pushed back. You couldn't consider him the reckless type, just violent and vindictive, a beast who enjoyed every action as a personal pleasure. Chances are he ran over Ralph Dewald mercilessly and shot Max Burke, disappointed only that he hadn't killed him. I figured Alan Isbell to be behind the whole thing given Molloy's status as an "associate." But, in the end, what was it all about?

Burke had mentioned two names: Jack Dragna and Robert G. Thompson. One a criminal, the other a communist. Isbell had no identifiable source of income. Like Arthur Whitman, the rich man without verifiable resources caused me to think of a criminal enterprise. There might have been another answer, but it was highly unlikely. Then it occurred to me the FBI's involvement could just as easily mean a Communist plot of some sort. I wondered why anyone would target Wichita. Los Angeles or New York would be more impressive targets.

The dominoes started to fall into place. Even after the war, we still had a booming aircraft industry. Housing and resources were at a premium. People stood in line for a lot of items that were plentiful before the war. Unaware what it took, I imagined it to be easier to infiltrate governments and businesses in smaller cities like ours. A city councilman here, a district attorney there, and before you knew it new laws influenced how governments and businesses operated. This could cause the tide to turn.

I couldn't think of any specific item Debra Rose Nathan could have taken from Brooks Mellon's studio to warrant Dragna or Siegel or Lansky to go after her. If it was mob related, a plane with several men in dark suits and hats and limited conversation would have flown in and roamed around town gunning for her. There would be muscle and money and quick answers, perhaps a little bloodshed. It would have been over by now.

Inside of ten minutes, I knocked on Bradley Wolrebinski's door on Park Place. He was pleased to see me but completely taken off guard when I blurted out, "Communists."

"Well, I have certainly been called worse."

I charged in past him. It was the first time in our acquaintance it appeared I had more energy than him. Svetlana stuck her head out from behind the kitchen door. I waved her over eagerly, and we all sat in the parlor.

"Could there be an infiltration of Communists in Wichita?"

They looked at each other, not in surprise or amazement, but more out of intellectual speculation. The silence between them spoke volumes.

"The possibility always exists," Svetlana responded. It astonished me she spoke first. Bradley always intended to grab the spotlight. "First, you defeat the Nazis, next you worry about the Communists."

"But aren't you both from countries that embraced Socialism?" I just about asked for a political history lesson. I needed the clarity of understanding. These two were the best teachers.

"There is a distinct difference between Socialism and Communism, Harold." Bradley's voice came out soft and direct, more like a college professor and less like a profligate writer of pulp novels. His intellect was on par with John Kenneth Galbreath. "Socialism advocates for economic resources to be shared equally by the citizens. Everyone benefits across the board. In a Communist society, those resources are owned and controlled by the state. Communist governments have the capacity to be just as corrupt as others, even a democracy, depending on the nature of their leaders and their ultimate intentions."

"As a writer, Bradley, how would you imagine they would do it? You know, infiltrate and take over? An innocuous step or a grand gesture?"

"February 20, 1939. Madison Square Garden." I thought for a moment Svetlana referred to a boxing match or garish vaudeville show. "The German American Bund rally."

Bradley nodded in remembrance.

"It looked straight out of the Nazi's evil gatherings at Nuremburg. They claimed George Washington, of all people, would likely be friends with Hitler. They warned of a Jewish takeover of Hollywood and the banking industry and anything else of importance. They advocated for the United States to enter the war on the side of Germany. Unbelievable. But it happened."

"Okay, that was the Nazis," I responded. "They were evil. We know that."

"That same approach can work for the others as well," Bradley continued. "These people only know vague accusations and insinuations and violence. They have no need of backing up their assertions with anything remotely resembling facts. The spectacle takes the place of Truth. Just consider Stalin and his purges in the 20s and 30s. If you look hard enough, you will find various groups asking Americans what real advantages there were from the war. What did we gain? We are now actively helping to rebuild the same Europe that we bombed. People are asking why do we even bother." He paused, maybe to gather his thoughts or perhaps for dramatic effect. "As I see it, there would be a dramatic event, an assassination or act of sabotage. The blame would fall on someone or some opposing group, maybe even the current administration. And if not the existing government, then simply a scapegoat. A small group significant enough to eradicate but large enough that citizens could consider as harmful."

"Like Jews?" I asked naively.

"Jews. Coloreds. Catholics. At that point, the Communists step in to claim a leadership role. Identify themselves as the true saviors of America. That they alone can make it great once again. It is all about getting a foot in the door."

"And then?"

"Once these extremists have control of even one small government or ruling body, their madness can spread. From a city to a county to a state."

"And then an entire country," Svetlana added on, with a sadness I had not known from her before.

I sat there blankly and stared at them, or rather between them. What could the target be? What could be dramatic enough to allow a group to claim to be social and political saviors? And what was the item stolen from the Mellon studio that caused such a concern?

"The Fourth of July," I blurted out. "Two days from now. The epitome of American patriotism. Lots of events going on. But which one?"

Bradley got the Sunday newspaper which contained a list of happenings in and around the city.

"Parade. Boat race on Lake Afton. Fireworks at Lawrence Stadium." Bradley read a list without emotion or speculation. I didn't get any hints from his inflection nor from the details.

"Any bigwigs, important people planning on visiting the city or giving a speech?"

"Phil Manning, the mayor."

"What about Governor Schoeppel?"

"Hmm, not that I can see."

I got up, ran my fingers through my hair, and paced around their parlor.

"This is crazy. Maybe there are Communists in Wichita and maybe they've got an event planned for the Fourth of July other than a picnic. Maybes. I've got a bunch of maybes."

Svetlana got up and came over to me. She stood in front of me, her hands on my shoulders. Her green eyes glowed with a regal majesty. Immediately, the tension left my body. My heart slowed to a normal pace. I breathed without hyperventilating.

"*To do justice and judgment is more acceptable to the Lord than sacrifice.*" For so long, Svetlana Halonen had always been the flighty artist, the woman who walked on clouds with her head even higher than that. She was, at that moment, a calm reassuring angel.

"There is someone who knows exactly what is going on, and they would rather I walk around with a target on my back than be Joshua and fight. Well, I am not a sheep."

My strength was restored. I turned and hugged Svetlana, walked over to Bradley and did the same. I left without a further word. Whatever I thought needed to remain within my heart only.

At the police station, a patrolman told me Gunny had left for the day after he worked an earlier shift. I went down to his house on East Zimmerly, right off Main Street straight down south from his job. It was a small house with one bedroom and one bathroom, just enough for him and his wife Olive. There had been many times we sat for a game of cribbage in the early days of my law enforcement career. He was the mentor who taught me more than the academy. He showed me the difference between sight and vision. In essence, a policeman's rabbi.

It was time to lay it all out, especially since this just might be far more than a missing girl. I had a duty as a responsible citizen to report the possibility of an attack of some sort. I also considered it wouldn't be a stretch of the imagination for me to come across as a deranged madman given the uncertainty and lack of specifics.

Floyd Gunsaullus was not the type to make rash judgments or even quick comments. A lot had transpired since the day Donald Long came to my door, a lot of players in this almost Shakespearean tragedy. He looked down at his hands folded in front of him. It took a full minute before he said a word.

"If this were coming from anyone else but you, Harold, I would dismiss it in a heartbeat." I started to speak, but he held his hand up, like a traffic safety cop. "But I've never known you to go off to Oz with wild theories."

"What about Whitman?"

"I half believed you then. But that was different. I just knew we didn't have any proof."

"So, what about this? Can you contact the FBI?"

"They'll deny they even have any agents here. Hoover is not the kind of guy that involves the local authorities. Not since the days of the gangsters. The press as well as his supervisors burned him several times while tracking Dillinger and those hoodlums. Besides, he wants to get all the glory and be America's hero. Don't you read the papers?"

"Yeah, but I haven't seen Hoover in the comics."

I got up in frustration and started to pace. In my head, I could hear a timer tick as though a bomb would go off somewhere at some time soon. The real one was still out there.

"What do we do?" I asked when I finally stopped pacing.

"Well, we typically have more units on patrol. There have already been a few accidents. It has given the men the Fourth jitters. But for the most part, we're prepared for anything."

"Even an act of sabotage? Or an assassination?"

"Look, Boeing is still on tight security, just like during the war. As far as an assassination, who could be a target whose death would make that much of an impact?"

"Anybody. It's not the who but how these people turn such an act into the key for their purposes."

Gunny believed me and respected me. But he had that cop's need for evidence. While he had allowed gut instinct in the past for his veteran officers, the desperation I exhibited did not meet that standard. There were too many "maybes" and "what-ifs" along with a high level of the unknown. If I took the time to listen to myself, I would have recognized that sooner.

He appreciated my feedback, said he would make a few phone calls, and get back to me if anything turned up. I thanked him and left. For now, all I could do was run around like a chicken with my head cut off and hope the Federal agents protected me before that happened.

Dorothy Martin popped back into my head. She came across as official and by the book. If that were the case, she really didn't have to approach me and warn me off or encourage me to continue my involvement. That meeting led me to believe they needed me, just not in an official capacity. I needed to know where she stayed.

I found a drug store near the corner of Zimmerly and South Broadway. I called Eileen at the Beacon switchboard. After some quaint conversation with one of her co-workers, she patched me through.

"Remember that art gallery curator at Isbell's?"

"The one from Pittsburgh? Yeah."

"You talked to her for a bit before I came out of my meeting with Isbell. Did she happen to mention what hotel she was at?"

Silence lay on the line for about fifteen seconds before Eileen blurted out in excitement.

"Yeah. She said because of last-minute travel plans, she couldn't get a reservation at the Broadview or the Pacific and had to stay at a smaller place called the Plaza Court Motel. I believe it might be down on—"

"South Broadway."

"Yeah."

"You're a doll."

I hung up, then stepped out onto the sidewalk. I looked up the block, just past the railroad tracks on the west side of the ride. I saw the Plaza Court Motel.

Now maybe I could get some answers.

Chapter Twenty-five

I parked just south of the Plaza Motor Court on Broadway, walked up the sidewalk briskly, but then turned slowly into the parking lot. There it was: the gray two door Nash parked in front of one of the back units partially obscured by the front office that faced the street. A half-hearted effort to be covert. At this point, I figured the notion of these accommodations because she couldn't get a room at the Broadview was the bunk. FBI agents don't stay in glamorous hotels, order room service, and throw their weight around. Plus, she mentioned other agents meandering around town. For all I knew, that might be malarkey as well. These folks were so secretive they likely had trouble recognizing each other.

The knock was more like a gentle rap. I hoped she would think it was one of her colleagues with an update. The door knob turned slightly, almost hesitantly. Momentarily, a brief crack showed in the door. With my shoulder and foot, I pushed my way in, in lieu of an invitation. Unfortunately, I absentmindedly used my bad foot, the one shot up in the war. The throbbing pain started almost instantaneously. I had to put that out of my mind because there were bigger issues at stake.

Dorothy Martin fell backward. I closed the door behind me and stood over her. Her eyes darted feverishly. I guessed she looked for her gun, although by now she could have assumed I was not the threat.

"I want answers," I demanded in a soft tone.

"You're not entitled to them," she responded defiantly.

I reached out to offer a hand to help her up. She slapped it away. I reached again. She finally took it. As she straightened out her skirt and smoothed her hair, she gave the appearance of a tough Virginia Mayo, only not blonde. She sat on the edge of the bed. She looked like a petulant child. An unappealing pout removed any notion of professionalism. Bested by a former policeman, an injured veteran, and a Jew likely turned her stomach sour.

"You're after Isbell?"

"Yes."

"Communists?"

"Something like that."

"What are they up to?"

"I don't know."

I looked at her incredulously. I found it difficult to accept the FBI would go to the trouble to send a squad of agents, one of them undercover, to get close to a mob and have no idea what they were up to. Maybe Hoover played things off the cuff.

"Please tell me the feds aren't using crystal balls now." Sure, thick sarcasm swam in my voice, but the thought of being out in the cold as a clay pigeon with no rhyme or reason rankled me.

"We've had our eye on Brooks Mellon for months. Fencing stolen goods and stag photos were of no interest to us. When he started meeting with a, shall we say, certain group, that was when we took notice. It meant he had stepped up his game."

"How does Debra Rose Nathan fit into all this?"

"She doesn't."

My jaw nearly hit the floor.

"I've got a mother sick to death over her missing daughter. And you sit there and tell me her disappearance has nothing to do with Isbell and his group?"

"There was nothing in Mellon's studio worth taking, except her nudie photos. But that Hephaestus Society thinks it might be incriminating shots of their meetings presumably taken by Mellon as insurance. This is why they're desperate for it. As of now, they're still an unknown quantity. They want to remain that way."

"Why don't you arrest these people?"

"For what? You used to be a police officer. We have no evidence of any illegal activities. Suspicion and hearsay don't find their way into the Justice Department's inquiries."

"Dewald is dead. Run over by a massive car. Someone shot Max Burke."

"And you can prove they did it?"

The black-and-white clarity stared me in the face. The law had specific parameters. Justice could only occur once the process went through a step-by-step basis. This was the issue I had. That and the fact a young girl played the part of a doe in the woods stalked by vicious hunters.

She nodded her head, perhaps in disgust or disappointment.

"What?" I asked bluntly.

"He said you'd cooperate because you were Jewish. That you knew how bad this could get."

"Who?"

"My boss. Alex Gordon. He's Jewish as well. Was

here in Kansas back in 1943. A town called Arkansas City."

"They pronounce it Ar-Kansas," I replied, annoyed at the anecdote.

"He knew what it was like to be a Jew in the FBI and then coming here. Back then, the locals helped him out. Beat cop named Baron Witherspoon."

The name popped in my head like a jack-in-the-box. As a second-year police officer in 1938, we experienced the Wichita Ripper. The detectives on that case were perplexed enough to call in Officer Witherspoon because he handled a similar case years earlier. I met him briefly, unfazed by the scarred face, a reminder of his experiences in the First World War. In one brief conversation, he suggested I keep my nose to the grindstone and disregard anyone who would stand in the way of my dreams.

Now, Dorothy Martin's boss was certain I would be cooperative merely because he and I were both Jewish. It just made me wonder how the government functioned. All these memories were nothing more than a distraction. For a moment, I felt sorry for Dorothy Martin when I forgot she had a directive she unflinchingly accepted.

"Is that it?" My tone was harsh, irritated, and fed-up.

"No." She had the look of acquiescence, her head hung, her voice almost tender. "General Carl Spaatz was just appointed Commanding General of the Army Air Forces in February. There is talk of creating an official and separate United States Air Force. This will add to our strength as a military force throughout the world. General Spaatz is in the middle of an unannounced tour of several facilities around the country to drum up support."

"Don't tell me. He's coming to Wichita."

"He's here. Today he tours Boeing. Tomorrow, he'll be at the Wichita Army Airfield to do an inspection of the 4156th AAF Base Unit. He's expressed interest in attending the fireworks display at Lawrence stadium on the fourth."

"Great. Just great. I've got to believe the Hephaestus Society likely found out about this somehow."

"Yes, it is a likely probability. If anything happens to the general it could easily be used to political advantage by Isbell's group. Blame could be placed on anarchists or a faction of subversives. He, or someone of name recognition, could step up and gain elective office."

She didn't need to go on. I started to pace. It had become a new habit, one done out of uncertainty with no real benefit. My job, the case I focused on, centered on a missing girl. I never considered it would become an issue of national security. I hated the fact this sidetracked me.

"Do the commanders of the Army Corp know about this?"

"Director Hoover believes army intelligence has their own protocols to follow and doesn't want to get into a jurisdictional fight. It might impact the general's initiative."

"You people are letting a decorated general and a young girl stand in the middle of nowhere because you want to avoid a jurisdictional fight? That is pretty cold, lady."

"I have my orders." A slight crack in her voice gave away her true feelings. A dedicated agent, she knew this was wrong.

All I could do was leave. Gunny had indicated the local police stepped up patrols but had nothing viable to go on. An FBI agent hoped a group of Communists would expose themselves and allow J. Edgar Hoover to stick another feather in his cap. I knew no one in the legitimate world of law and order who had any motivation or compelling argument to stop what could likely be a runaway train. That left only the misfits whose primary incentive was money.

I drove north, back to the Red Apple. I entered but stayed by the front door. Tyler Schenkel saw me. I left and waited by my car on the other side of the gas pump. In about a minute, he ambled over to me as though he didn't have a care in the world. Maybe he didn't.

"I want to hire you," I said.

He laughed like he read the funny papers. The thought was far too comical to take seriously. Then he stopped laughing.

"For what?" His face didn't move, not a muscle. It was a block of stone. The joke wasn't funny anymore.

"Bodyguard."

"Who?"

"General Carl Spaatz."

He stared at me, tried to read my face, my voice, translate my words from the possibly ridiculous to him into a viable business arrangement that would be far more appealing. For all his spunk, he didn't have a clue.

"What gives, Bergman?"

"The general is going to the Fourth of July fireworks at Lawrence Stadium. I have information that leads me to believe someone might to try to kill him."

"So. Why should I care?"

"Because if he is killed, it will be the start of a major

transformation in this country. One in which guys like you and me don't stand a chance."

"We don't walk on the same side of the street, remember?"

I put a hand on his shoulder. It might have been a daring move, but I had no other choice.

"Doesn't matter. They'll just close up the street all together."

He stared at me. The two of us were army veterans, both of us impacted by our service in the war. Mine was physical and moral. His perhaps deeper. We went about our lives in a far different manner than each other, the only desire to survive until the next day. Perhaps he tried to figure life out just like me, only he came to different conclusions and used different methods. We were the flip side to the same coin.

"What do you get for working cases?" he asked me.

"Twenty-five dollars a day plus expenses."

"All right. I'll take that."

I outlined what I needed him to do which was, when I sounded it out, very minimal. On the day of the fireworks, he needed to find and tail the general and his entourage but stay as out of sight as possible. If he noticed anything glaringly suspicious, he was to call the police. If necessary, he could do it anonymously. Overall, he was pleased at the idea of getting paid to be a birdwatcher.

I knew he didn't have the same skills as I, so it would be relatively easy to keep an eye on him to determine who might be on his tail. This turned out to be a tangled mess as several people watched many others, a Mobius strip of hunters and hunted where the events were indistinguishable and patterns undifferentiated. I never really considered someone like Alan Isbell to be in the middle of these kind of things. They were too messy for someone of his ilk. My target was Zach Molloy, the one with the greatest ability to kill or maim. I looked for a chance to put him down like a rabid dog.

Max Burke, true to his word, had checked out of the hospital against the doctor's recommendation. I found this out when I stopped off at the Lexington Hotel. He had poured himself a stiff drink just as I stepped through the door. The way he moved about slowly told me he was still in a lot of pain. The grimace quickly changed into a friendly smile. Like any dedicated performer, the show must go on.

I outlined everything for him, including the presence of the FBI and the possibility of a high-ranking general in line for assassination. He listened to me carefully, nodded at each major point of information, and commented only minimally. From a big brute who choked down an impressive breakfast when we first met to now, I saw him in a far different light. Maybe he had some moxie after all. I had to hope he did. Neither of us could back out now.

"How do you think these guys are going to kill a military man in a stadium? They'll have a lot of security posted all around. Not to mention the soldiers that accompany the guy." Though I doubted he served in the armed forces, Burke spoke with a tactical clarity.

"If they bring down the whole stadium, that will do the trick. Won't it?"

"A bomb?"

"Police suspected Molloy had set bombs in the cars of two rival gangsters back in 1937. That was my first year on the force. Nobody could pin anything on him, but the detectives at the time determined he had the know-how to build those devices. Apparently, he has training as an electrical engineer."

"Pretty impressive for a thug."

"Quite."

"So, if he's wandering around the stadium, we've got our target."

"Oh, heck, Max. There are a million possibilities at this point. I can't be sure if General Spaatz is not a decoy and they'll try to poison the water treatment plant. This is the best we have to go on. A high-profile target and one that could be most impactful to their cause. I've got nothing else right now. God help us if I'm wrong."

It was as though I rode a carousel that had begun to spin faster. At that point, I couldn't get off. This might wind up the biggest shot in the dark I had ever been involved in. I had only my abiding faith in Adonai to see me through to a just end.

Chapter Twenty-six

Who watched who? If Army Intelligence were prepared, they would have a list of veterans like Tyler Schenkel who had drifted away from legitimate business. They would have identified their residences and known associates. They might have mug shots to identify anyone even remotely in the area. They couldn't arrest someone or hold them without due process and wouldn't involve local law enforcement. From Dorothy Martin, the FBI knew of my involvement and likely used me to get to the real perpetrators, since they probably had no deep infiltration into the Hephaestus Society beyond the cursory introduction at the recent benefit. Max Burke and I had to keep a close eye out for Zach Molloy as he was the main cog in the efforts at malfeasance. Unless, of course, someone else had been employed to do the job. In which case, we were chasing our own tails.

Still, the one question to answer in all this once the dust had settled: Where was Debra Rose Nathan? I had a few guesses. She might easily have been located early on, kidnapped with the stag film in hand, and held once it was determined no conclusive evidence against the Hephaestus Society existed. It was just as easy to eliminate her as an unwitting pawn in a bigger game. Murder didn't seem like a chance these people would take, except if was expedient or necessary. I hadn't yet determined their level of desperation.

215

As with all journeys of faith, it was necessary to follow the path unto the end, not fear the cobblestones beneath your feet or the vultures that soared above your head. I took a deep breath and Psalms 91:11 came into my mind: "*For he shall give his angels charge over thee, to keep thee in all thy ways.*" I had to believe it was so.

As of now, I had to assume Tyler Schenkel kept a surreptitious eye on the general as he went off for an inspection at the air base. Therefore, Max and I drove around the city for two reasons. The first, to reconnoiter Lawrence Stadium in terms of access and possible placement of some kind of ordnance. My military background would hopefully be enough to identify such a location. Additionally, I needed to use my status as a target to my advantage. I figured there was a good chance both the FBI and Isbell's followers kept track of us. As we ambled around the city, Max and I could take note of any strange vehicles that paid particular attention to us.

The military had cordoned off the stadium both in preparation for the fireworks as well as the appearance of the general. The best we could do was circle around twice along West Maple Street and South Sycamore Street because they'd closed off McLean Boulevard. We had to drive slow enough to take a good look and a good guess but not so slow that any official personnel would notice and suspect us. There were three primary points we could calculate with minimal effort and focused our attention there.

We had the audacity to drive by the Plaza Court Motel to find the Nash not parked. We also drove by Isbell's house a couple of times, just to make our presence known. We took a good long lunch at Droll's

English Grill. I considered the possibility Molloy would stop in and our appearance could ruffle his feathers. I had no illusions we could scare these people into divulging their plans. They were intent upon domination of the country, perhaps even the world. A gruff character from LA and a Jewish private detective from Wichita were certainly no match for that. We just needed to be good enough.

My mind wandered desperately as I tried to consider where Debra Rose Nathan could be. It would make sense if she stole inappropriate photos which someone mistook for a more valuable item. However, there were a few aspects that didn't gel.

I had Max recount what he knew about her association with Brooks Mellon. He started with her first appearance at the studio and then through all the sessions he knew her to be involved in.

From there I calculated a timeline. The girl had returned almost two months ago, around the first week of May. Donald Long came to visit me on June eighteen. Even if she had disappeared only a week before, that made it a solid month she had been home. By Max Burke's account, Mellon's death occurred either the last week of May or first week of June.

Mellon would have known shortly after the girl's departure that an item of importance was stolen. If it were only the stag photos, he might not have been concerned. However, if it had any relevance to this group of Communist sympathizers, the events would have taken place earlier. Max Burke would have come to Wichita sooner. The girl might be missing before Donald Long's visit. I determined the events in Los Angeles had nothing to do with her disappearance here in Wichita.

Burke's assumptions led me down this path that happened to cross with the interests of national security. What you would call the apex of irony.

While I felt duty bound to proceed as planned, the girl's disappearance now seemed to have nothing to do with any of this. Little bits and pieces floated around in my head. A previous encounter and an earlier conversation resonated in my mind.

We drove around town during the evening hours and caught a few shenanigans as kids lit off fireworks. I ran into a Patrolman Urban Steinke, recently graduated from the academy, who filled us in on a Wichita bus driver who got his right arm singed when a kid tossed a firecracker into the vehicle. He shook his head and second-guessed his career choice.

At Max's suggestion, we passed by the Plaza Court Motel and found the Nash parked there. A black four-door Chevy sedan parked alongside it. My guess is the FBI agents mapped out a plan for the Fourth. Burke elbowed my shoulder.

"You want to crash the party?"

I chuckled.

"As much as I'd like to, I think we better just let them carry out their assignment. Might be helpful to us in the end."

I looked in the rearview mirror with a certain degree of concern.

"What?" Burke asked.

"Well, there's another black four-door that's been tailing us since we left with that patrolman."

"Yeah, I know."

"Why haven't you said anything?"

"I figured you knew what you were doing."

I was ready to drop Burke off for the night, but he wanted to stop at the Surf Lounge for a nightcap, his treat. He considered it the closest thing he had come across in Wichita to Los Angeles. The place was tacky and made me think I wouldn't enjoy Los Angeles.

"What if we're wrong?" His voice sounded desperate. I initially thought he might be disappointed about missing out on a good payout.

"Look, you've got the FBI in town crawling all over the place. There is Army Intelligence as well as the general's staff and aides. Putting the future of democracy on our shoulders alone is too much of a burden to bear."

He shot down his drink, and then flagged down the waitress for another while I sipped mine.

"I don't like it. I didn't get involved with these shenanigans to be a Medal of Honor winner."

As soon as he said it, my thoughts flew to Dick Cowin. Both of us from Wichita, but different basic training units, and only encountered each other in Europe. We compared notes about life. I was the first Jewish guy he'd ever met. My injuries came two days before he was killed in action. It took me several weeks to learn of his passing. His folks asked me to accompany them to the White House where President Truman presented them with the award posthumously. When I considered Dick's life and his exploits, I realized none of us signed up to be heroes. It is simply thrust upon you. Either you accept it, or you don't. Most times, you don't get a choice.

"I know why you got involved, Burke. Chances are there is nothing in it for you in terms of dollars and cents. You could have backed out earlier. So, why didn't you?"

The waitress placed Burke's drink down in front of

him. He simply stared at it.

"To tell you the truth, I don't know."

He finished the drink in one hard gulp, stood up, and threw enough bills on the table to cover the tab. I didn't go after him. All men, of whatever ilk, come to a certain point where they determine the best course of action whether they regard it as so. Maybe that just happened with Max Burke. I didn't know him well enough to figure it. I believed he would be standing upright if and when the bullets flew.

I drove home as I realized I had to make amends with the cats for my absence from the apartment all day. I immediately crouched down with the intention of scratching ears and rubbing bellies, only to fall over while Lady Mittens and Sir Pounce covered my chest and legs. I encountered a bit of demonstrative meowing which I took to be a kind of feline remonstrance. After their due diligence, they got off me and marched over to the pantry where I quickly took out a can of food and divided it into two bowls. The meowing ceased as gratified eating commenced.

While they feasted, I started a kettle to make a cup of tea to go along with the almond cookies Mrs. Hanover had baked for me. I needed to compose myself and my thoughts and consider the next day.

By the time I woke up tomorrow, I would need to disregard the FBI, the army personnel, and even the Wichita Police Department. My main objective was Zach Molloy. He had the skills to accomplish a bombing and the apparent trust of Alan Isbell, the presumed leader of this endeavor. There might be others in this organization but at this time I did not know who they were, nor did I have the time to determine that.

Max had a valid point when he asked about our efforts if we failed. Throughout history, there had been times when it seemed that evil had conquered. I understood it was only temporary. The forces of Good always transpired eventually. For one of the rare moments in my life, I thought not of the future or the past. This time, right now, was all that mattered.

I found a degree of irony in that a search for a missing young girl turned into a battle fit for Joshua. How had I found myself in this position? A man with a limp who opted not to carry a gun in a profession that dictated its use. A man who respected both the laws of man and the laws of God and yet travelled the middle road. One who saw the brief glimpses of light in the shadow as well as the clouds as they approached on a sunny day.

I was not so vain as to consider myself a prophet or judge. I spoke better than Moses but still had flaws. I suppose all of us who recognize our humanity know that. It was the vain who were wicked and destined to fall.

No, Max need not be concerned. If we were true to ourselves and true to our beliefs, we can never fail. Svetlana's words from Proverbs 21:3 rang in my ears yet again: "*To do justice and judgment is more acceptable to the Lord than sacrifice.*"

Chapter Twenty-Seven

It would have been easy and far more prudent to simply walk down to King's X and start off the day with a hearty breakfast. I realized I needed to stay focused, sit in silence without distraction, and eliminate the interference from the outside world. Naturally, the cats advised me otherwise in their own fashion, but their attention-seeking was less intrusive than a random person who made meaningless chit-chat.

I fixed some scrambled eggs and toast, one pot of coffee, and sat at my meager dining table with my notebook. I went over all the memos I had scribbled down over the last several days and tried to pinpoint the possibilities. Strangely, with all that had gone on, I never once thought of Debra Rose Nathan, the object of my investigation. Donald Long and Arlene Nathan were the reasons I started a journey that took me to a higher place. Not that a missing girl was not important, but she simply became the reason all this began. I had to be certain it would all come back around to her at some point, as is the very nature of faith.

It didn't start out as a typically hot July day, but I sensed it would get that way by midday. The air thick with humidity made my skin heavy, and the winds had only started to increase by the time I got down to King's X to pick up Max Burke. He had a self-satisfied smile on his face as he wiped his mouth and dipped his napkin in his water glass to clean his hands. A slight belch followed.

"Your girl, Jennie, took good care of me," he burbled. "I'm ready to hunt bear."

What a city boy from California knew about hunting bear was beyond me. I figured they all spoke that way out there. A little jive and gibberish.

We needed to locate Tyler Schenkel and keep an eye on him while we remained as open as possible to draw out the FBI, the Hephaestus society, or anyone else who mattered. We took the dual roles of hunter and hunted. If all went as planned, there would eventually be a confluence of all the interested parties, with us hopefully coming out on top. Robert Burns once commented about the plans of mice and men.

There were several events along the Arkansas River. Men in shirt sleeves and ladies in summer dresses walked along the banks. Kids either skimmed stones, tried to fly kites, or simply ran around and whooped it up to keep with the spirit of the day. It all looked innocent, typical for this time of year in Wichita, Kansas. What most folks had no knowledge of was the undercurrent of evil that permeated below the surface. Only cops and criminals were aware of such dealings, as well as a couple of guys who wouldn't normally be privy to these matters.

On Douglas Avenue in front of the Pacific Hotel, I ran into Patrolman Ronald Saub. He had twenty years in, pushing close to retirement. We got along well as we discussed various aspects of Jewish life before I enlisted. I hadn't seen him since my return. He looked a spell older.

"Enjoying the festivities or something else?" He

looked at me suspiciously. I half wondered whether Gunny had informed the patrolmen that I worked a case.

"A little of both, Ronnie."

I couldn't tell if he responded with a smile of awareness or a smirk of confusion.

The lunch crowd had cleared out by the time we got to the Pan American. King Mar jokingly castigated me for my extended absence. The serious look on my face let him know it was not personal. At that, he asked if he could do anything. This was far too big to get him involved, too dangerous for him to risk his neck. He would have, without hesitation, due to the nature of our friendship. I just didn't want to let him step into the fray this time.

The purpose of this early afternoon meandering was to see who might be on our tail. A couple of different black four-door Chevies had taken turns, but the gray Nash was nowhere in sight. Additionally, I wasn't sure how many FBI agents besides Dorothy Marion were in town. She hadn't let on anything in that regard. At this point, anyone we saw could be an advocate or an enemy.

Burke and I headed for the Army Air Base. Our route took us past the Plainview neighborhood and the Boeing facilities. I had no need to try to visit Arlene Nathan as we were not at liberty to discuss our endeavors. Also, I found no desire on my part to have to explain how this had to do with her daughter. To anyone, it would appear so far off the mark. Heck, I often wondered how it got to this place. In the end, I hoped and prayed it would all work out.

An old beige two-door Ford coupe parked behind a telephone pole a couple of hundred feet from the front entrance to the base. I recognized it as Schenkel's car.

He often claimed he wasn't about showing off anything except a bankroll, the only thing that identified where you stood in life. I guess to each his own.

I stopped the car. Burke and I waited and watched. I glanced in the rearview mirror, saw the gray Nash approach and then pass, and eventually disappear from sight. We couldn't figure out for sure what she was up to. At the very least, we knew she was out and about. By midafternoon, a group of official cars emerged from the main entrance to the base, led and followed by Army officers on motorcycles. From our perch on North Oliver, we watched them drive west on Thirty-First Street, presumably heading back toward downtown. The last motorcycle officer stopped when he saw the Ford. Schenkel started his car, turned suddenly, and drove past us, while the officer pulled out a notebook and wrote down some notations, likely the license tag, before he caught up with the convoy. I was fairly confident the military guys had everything they needed to protect their VIP. Then again, you never knew what the enemy had planned.

It got to be twilight. Burke declined the opportunity to get dinner somewhere before things started to get interesting. He focused on our actions in a manner I had not seen up until now. Maybe it was all personal to him, a sense of professional integrity he had let go of in the past that now came back. Reclaiming the character he had before he sold out for cold hard cash. Then again, he might have had a plan on how he could make a buck out of this after all.

We circled our way back to Lawrence Stadium. The day started to drag now. Waves at the beach worked the same way. Nothing happened for a long time. The ocean pulls back, gathers up strength, and then comes crashing down. The idea is to be prepared for it, so the undertow doesn't carry you away.

The general's convoy arrived at the stadium. We were on Sycamore Street, a block away south of West Maple. From that vantage point, we saw the Ford come down from Delano to the north.

A group of soldiers on guard duty approached the vehicle. It tried to back up but faced a soldier who pointed a rifle at the back window. We witnessed Schenkel as they pulled him from the car and handcuffed him. While I hoped Schenkel might make a good bodyguard, my thought all along was to use him as an unwitting diversion, without, of course, letting him know. That would have ruffled his feathers. It worked.

A maintenance man of some kind with dark brown coveralls and heavy boots crossed the street at West Maple from the opposite side of the stadium. He made his way to the southwest corner where support beams created a kind of cavern. The man was tall and dark haired. He carried a small black tool case. I recognized him immediately: Zack Molloy.

We pulled up and turned east onto West Maple. I turned into the parking lot. Burke and I got out of the car quickly and circled around from opposite sides to where we saw him enter the area. Burke assured me he wouldn't draw his gun unless absolutely necessary. We both knew the presence of the military would have made it a shoot-first-ask-questions-later situation. We just had to hope we were in a position to answer those questions.

It was a bad time for my foot to start to throb. However, I had no control over it. Burke, as well, seemed weighed down by both his breakfast and lunch. He was also a heavyset man not prone to aggressive chases. On top of that, he had been shot only a couple of days ago and had mostly hidden his discomfort. For those reasons, Molloy easily raced between us, back across the street, and into his car.

He took off west on Maple toward Seneca, then north. We followed closely.

I pushed the car hard, uncertain of how much it could take.

Molloy turned left on Burton, a quick right on Elizabeth, before a sudden left back onto Burton. Due to his speed on the sharp turns, his car seemed to slide in that intersection. He accelerated when he made a sharp turn north onto South Glenn Avenue, lost control after we went over the railroad tracks there, skidded, and turned over twice, before the car smacked against a tall pine tree and landed in a clump of grass. The wheels spun and an acrid smoke filled the air.

We were less than thirty seconds behind. The car was a wreck. Pinned against the steering wheel, Zack Molloy had a bloodied face and a look of agony in his eyes. He experienced the pain he had inflicted on others. It wasn't exactly the retribution described in Exodus but it would suffice for now.

"Get me out of here," he screamed in anguish like an animal shot during a hunt.

Burke and I stood over him, arms crossed in a posture of malaise.

"We could. Couldn't we, Max?"

"I suppose so, Harold."

No one would mistake us for Abbott and Costello.

"Did you set a bomb?" I asked him bluntly. He grimaced in a sad effort to extricate himself. "Did you set a bomb?" I repeated, enunciating each word.

"Yes," he blurted angrily. "Timed. Nine thirty. Right after the general's speech when the first fireworks go off."

Burke looked at his wristwatch.

"That gives us twenty minutes."

I leaned down close to Molloy, quite satisfied that Goliath had fallen in front of me. I made sure not to be too prideful at this success. That would be a greater sin.

"Names, Molloy. You're going to give us names. And testify."

"Anything. Just get me out of here."

We did not use the gentility of ambulance drivers or doctors. Burke surprised me with a set of handcuffs. He and Molloy rode in the back seat. While we drove back to the stadium quickly. We went into the same parking area as the general and were approached by the same soldiers that had stopped Schenkel, but convinced them of the scenario. Given the time factor, evacuating the stadium was impossible. Fortunately, Molloy had the sense to advise how to disarm the bomb which involved cutting a wire to an alarm clock. As it turns out, he valued his own hide over that of any of his employers. Especially when he was closer to the bomb about to go off and they were well out of range, likely enjoying a few cocktails in College Hill.

Just as we finished, a black four-door Chevy arrived. The passenger showed his credentials to the officer in charge, who looked at the remainder of his detail with a certain degree of uncertainty and apprehension. A moment of hesitation wafted over the confrontation before they acquiesced and allowed them to take Molloy away. The credentials must have been enough to convince.

The gray Nash parked across the street, nearly in the same spot Molloy had been. I wasn't sure how long it had been there. The driver never got out. Burke and I had to unceremoniously answer questions without a rescue by Dorothy Martin. Our credentials did not afford us the same luxury of an expedient departure.

A detail escorted the general from the stadium before the fireworks began, while the detail questioned us. Forty-five minutes later, the fireworks show ended, the army officers were satisfied with our answers, and allowed us to leave. The gray Nash watched the whole thing. I could only hope the entire scene amused her.

I drove from the stadium parking lot across the street. As I got out of the car, I told Burke to wait for a moment. I was silently summoned. I got into the passenger side.

"What's the matter? Didn't you want to come to my rescue?" I asked playfully.

"The army took care of the general. We got what we wanted."

"I assume you'll go after Isbell next?"

"Already done." She wore a satisfied smirk while I sat confused by her response. "Don't ask. This is not part of your jurisdiction." Was her smile related to the case or me still in the dark and her still in charge? Either way, she made it clear I didn't need to ask.

I allowed myself to be content with this resolution. America was safe, for the moment. I still had the matter of a missing girl which I knew the FBI had no interest in nor would assist in a resolution despite their resources. A few ideas had crossed my mind of late, and I would follow up on them very soon.

"So, that's it then?" I asked.

She handed me an envelope. It appeared thick and heavy.

"You were likely unaware, but the government offered a five-thousand-dollar reward for any information leading to the capture of a Communist ring that had infiltrated the Midwest. I believe you deserve this."

I held the envelope in my hand; my fingers squeezed as though grabbing a knish at a bar mitzvah.

"Typically, there is a lot of paperwork associated with rewards of this nature. Government bureaucracy can often take time to get these issues resolved."

"Is that so?"

I was dubious, but pleased.

"This is a special type of reward, Mr. Bergman. Call it the no-questions-asked kind. You know, the one where we thank you for your service to your country and ask you to keep your big mouth shut about it."

She smiled at me. It was ironic to hear such demonstrative words come from a warm and gentle face. It wasn't necessary to question any further or put up a sanctimonious front. It wouldn't have done much good anyway. Rewards, like blessings, come in many forms. I nodded and stepped out of the car. She drove off to places unknown as she continued to keep the country safe from threats most citizens knew nothing about and wouldn't believe if they did.

"What was that all about?" Burke inquired sleepily.

"It seems we have been honored as forthright American patriots who now have a little extra gelt in our pockets."

Burke smiled, uncertain of the Yiddish expression, but almost assured it meant he came out ahead.

Chapter Twenty-Eight

Max Burke initially wanted to fly back to Los Angeles in style, first class with preferential treatment by the stewardesses. Eat high quality food and drink champagne. Smoke a foul cigar while most of the plane grew nauseous. Then he reconsidered the financial expenditure and time, multiple connections and over a hundred and twelve dollars for the fare, before he realized he was quite happy to spend forty-eight dollars and thirteen cents to take the Atchison Topeka and Santa Fe in the railroad's version of first class. He also had to consider there would be more room in a sleeper car than an airplane seat.

We got to Union Station earlier than Burke preferred, but he figured he had no further need or desire to hang around Wichita. He politely inquired as to whether he might be useful helping me look for the girl. Ultimately, it was a gracious offer, one made with honest consideration. I indicated he was better off on the West Coast.

"And be careful of Detective Sergeant Noone. He's got it in for you."

"He owes me a hundred bucks from a card game he shouldn't have been at," Burke responded with a laugh. "You know, with all this cabbage in my pocket, I just might let him off the hook."

We shook hands warmly. I had come to respect him

in a manner of speaking. While he didn't seem to enjoy his time in Kansas quite as much, he handled himself and the matter of the Communists with a kind of professional integrity. I only smiled when he departed with a vague invitation for me to come visit him in California.

My next stop was at police headquarters, early enough for me to catch someone from the Night Detective Squad. I found Frank Parson. If you met him, you knew better than to call him by his given name of Francis. He was just a couple of months older than me, but the cases he worked made him seem a whole lot older. The lines on his forehead were indicative of a pensive thinker.

"Hey, Frank."

"Harold."

"You got anything on a Jeremy Thatcher?"

"Let me look."

He left to go to the file room, and I waited in the detectives' room for about fifteen minutes. Parson came back in whistling impressively.

"What is it?" I asked incredulously.

"He's one sandwich short of a picnic."

I understood the reference, just not how it pertained to Thatcher. There were multiple encounters with the police regarding vandalism, an accusation of arson in a wooded area around his home, and a violent outburst about a year ago in which his mother authorized the police to lock him up for twenty-four hours. I checked the date with my notebook and found it coincided with his senior prom.

"What is he capable of, Frank?"

"Well, he doesn't run around with a gang, otherwise we'd have him by now. We picked him up a couple of times for vandalism with a kid named Marky Miller. Now that kid was a real piece of work. Short, bully, a kind of Baby Face Nelson complex. You know? Always looking to pick a fight. I think that attitude encouraged Thatcher, egged him on. After all, couldn't tell which one was the leader and which the follower. Either way, the stuff in the file looks pretty bad. But, you know, I just can't figure with a kid like this. Maybe all he needs is direction."

That was likely an understatement.

"Anything since that lock up?" I asked.

"Nope."

"What about the Miller kid?"

"Haven't seen or heard anything about him. Kid like that is always in trouble with one beat cop or another."

"Think he left town?"

"Anything is possible."

Given Thatcher's mother was a cleaning woman who took in laundry and Jeremy went through various part-time jobs, his violent tendencies had a good opportunity to continue unabated. My mind tried to speculate how all this tied in to Debra Rose Nathan.

Then it struck me. Richie's words after he chatted with the kid. He had a big crush on the girl. Was highly disappointed when she went to California. It probably stuck in his mind she left him behind, just ran off and deserted him. Also, an avid collector of Cracker Jack prizes. Debra Rose's return was the biggest prize. He wasn't about to let her go again. It made sense, but just like with the Hephaestus Society, I had no proof.

My impassioned knock on Donald Long's apartment door yielded nothing. I drove quickly down to Arlene Nathan's house and miraculously found her. My eyes were wild, frantic, and I must have looked out of control. It was wrong of me to approach her in this fashion given the calm and reassuring demeanor I had presented each time before. She gasped and then started to breathe fast.

"How well do you know Jeremy Thatcher?" I blurted out.

"He and Debra Rose went to high school together. He might have hung around her there. Not sure really."

"Did he plan to take her to the prom?"

"Not that I know of."

"Did he see her when she came back from California?"

"I don't know."

"Has he come around here much?"

"Well, yes. Just about every day. Mr. Bergman, what is this all about?"

"His mother. Have you seen his mother recently?"

She was silent. My questions were like pieces of a jigsaw puzzle. They were slowly set into place. She couldn't handle the picture it created. She collapsed in her seat. I spoke to her calmly and finally got her to write down his address. I held her hands in mine. Without a word, my eyes gave her reassurance. I was Joshua. There were about to be walls tumbling down.

It was everything I could do to stop from racing at a high rate of speed. The notions churned in my head and made me realize the worst possible outcomes. We had all assumed this young man to be a sweet innocent kid. In truth, his wickedness was sheathed in innocence. The wolf in lamb's clothing.

From Taanit 23 I have read: "*Either a friend or death.*" My fear now was Jeremy Thatcher had no more friends.

The house stood well off South Clinton. While a few homes appeared to be built around the start of the war had nice lawns and flower beds, the Thatcher house was more ramshackle. It must have been around since the early part of the century when this was all farmland. It was a two-story house with white clapboards in great need of paint. I could see a storm shelter and imagined a root cellar of some sort in the vicinity, a feature of many houses of that period.

It was too late to contemplate my lack of a gun. My instincts were it wouldn't be necessary with Jeremy. He just didn't seem to be that type. The wild-eyed gangster. A new version of Two-Gun Crowley. Otherwise, there would have been several unsolved killings in this area the police would have known about. His vandalism and arson were more signs of a juvenile than a seasoned killer. I could be wrong. I hoped my instincts were right.

I knocked on the door lightly, stepped into the house, and called out his name pleasantly, as though it were a visit to a friend. There were dishes in the sink and a general appearance of a house not cleaned for quite some time. It made me shudder when I considered Thatcher's mother's presence was absent. I continued to call out his name, walked slowly, and stopped every so often to hear for any sounds. From the basement, I heard a bottle suddenly kicked.

A small light bulb at the door in the kitchen gave enough illumination to get down the stairs. What I would see once I got down there was anyone's guess. The dirt floor caused my foot to slip. This resulted in some pain in my ankle. It was too late to do anything about it.

At the base of the stairs stood a tall set of shelves

that had many jars of canned foods. To the right of the shelves were three wooden boxes stacked on each other. In the corner, a table with various tools on it: a hammer, an awl, a couple of screwdrivers, and a long wrench.

As I turned the corner, I saw Debra Rose Nathan as she sat on a wooden rocking chair, hands tied in front of her, mouth gagged, and with a look of sheer terror. Her eyes were red and puffy, the result of many tears over a long period of time. Her nose was runny, her hair in disarray. There were bruises on her neck. Whatever had transpired in Los Angeles could not compare to the last few weeks.

Candles burned on two small tables on either side of her. It gave the room an eerie aspect worse than Halloween. Jeremy stood behind her, a sharp knife in his hand held to her throat. I stopped and looked at him. I didn't need her to see my concern.

"You're not taking her from me," he said calmly, almost serenely. "She's mine."

"Has she accepted that, Jeremy?"

He looked down at the top of her head. He made no attempt to look her in the eyes. He knew the truth but could not accept staring it in the face.

"This is who I am." He seemed resigned to whatever fate had planned for him.

"No. Not completely." He looked at me like a lost puppy. *"Whether a man is strong or weak, rich or poor, wise or foolish, depends mostly on circumstances from before he was born. But whether a man is good or bad, righteous or wicked depends only on his own free will."*

I let that sink in for a moment. "You have the power to be merciful, Jeremy. Her life is in your hands. Remember that: Her life is in your hands."

His head dipped just slightly.

I thought I might have gotten to him, reached a piece of him that had been a sweet innocent kid at one time. Despite all the talking, his mother did not make an appearance. I thought of the possibilities but knew I needed to refocus my attention on this standoff. The present stood in front of me. I could not, at this moment, think of any future.

"She's mine," he repeated, this time through pursed lips and gritted teeth. "Go. You're not welcome here."

"Her mother is worried about her."

"Go!" he yelled. The stone walls seemed to shake.

Debra Rose shuddered.

I was the only thing that could prevent Jeremy from carrying out whatever his final plans were.

My hand had been on the edge of the table the entire time. Whatever I could manage to grab could be useful but if I weren't quick enough, Jeremy's knife would cut the girl's throat or stab her. If I could distract him by throwing something, I had about five or six feet of ground to cover with a throbbing foot that would slow me down. It seemed like a mile. Then again, according to the labor is the reward.

It was the wrench. I threw it across my body to strike the hand or arm that held the knife. It worked. Jeremy dropped the knife, and I immediately made up the ground before he realized what I did.

I threw my body at him. He went backward a further three feet and struck the back wall. I was a couple of feet away from him. We were both on the dirt floor.

For the moment, I saw him as a German soldier. This was some road in the countryside, some field in France, some patch of forest somewhere in Belgium. I had no Garand rifle available, no bayonet, just bare hands to fight an enemy. Certainly, at this point, it was to the death.

He started to get back up. From a crouching position, I catapulted myself into him. My shoulder caught him in the belly. A loud gasp indicated I had knocked the wind out of him.

His arm swung wildly and caught me on the side of my head. I was dazed but kept pressing on. I turned my body so that my torso pushed against him. I tried to keep my head away as best I could.

My last assault knocked him against the back wall again. He started to slump. I came across with a roundhouse to his chin. He went down.

Still groggy, I picked up the knife and cut Debra Rose Nathan loose from her bonds.

"Let's get you home."

We made it as far as my car before I dropped, dizzy and uncertain where I was. Her screams brought out a couple of the neighbors. Their phone calls resulted in an ambulance and the police. The day turned to darkness in a matter of moments.

There were several hours of stethoscopes and x-rays and thermometers. Dr. Enders at Wesley Medical Center indicated I had mostly bruises but requested to keep me overnight to check for a concussion. I politely declined his request.

Clarence Mendenhall came to visit as I put on my street clothes. His hat sat tipped back on his head, and he looked mighty pleased, this time not with himself.

"I've said it before and I'll say it again. You've got the makings to come back to the force as a full detective."

"What are you talking about?"

"We found Mrs. Thatcher in her bedroom, her arms crossed over her chest. She looked all nice and peaceful like."

"Dead?"

"Deader than Dillinger."

"Jeremy?" He nodded. "Why?"

"He blamed her for keeping him from going to the prom with the Nathan girl. You better believe those headshrinkers are gonna have a field day with that kid. Oh, and they found Marky Miller."

"Where?"

"Stuffed in a trunk. At least what was left of him." Now we knew the leader from the follower.

"What about the girl?"

"Shook up pretty bad. The doctors here checked on her. But she's back with her mom now. Lots of tears and hugs. I think she'll be okay. That Donald Long feller asked me to tell you to visit him soon as you were feeling okay."

Clarence balanced his praise for me with an admonition about my decision not to stay. All I did was give him a look. I got my tie on but left it loose around my neck. I had no desire to look spruced up since I didn't feel that way. Mendenhall and I started to leave, but I stopped for a moment.

"I appreciate what you said about me coming back. I really do. But this is the stuff that makes me uncomfortable."

"What do you mean?"

"Jeremy Thatcher killed his mother and kidnapped a girl. Those are undeniably crimes. Yet there is something wrong with him. He's not a petty criminal, a gangster, or even a bunch of Communists. Police think only of the law, of punishment. Someone like Jeremy makes me think of something else."

"Like what?"

"Repentance."

"Well, he'll have plenty of time to reflect on that up in Osawatomie."

Therein lay our differences.

On the way out, I stopped at the front desk and politely asked to use their phone. I caught Eileen at the switchboard at the Beacon. She was surprised to hear from me.

"Say, where are you calling from?"

"Wesley Medical Center."

"What are you doing there?"

"I'll tell you tomorrow night over dinner."

"Oh, where are we going?"

"My place."

"You're cooking?"

"Yes."

"Well, this should be interesting."

I couldn't agree with her more.

Chapter Twenty-Nine

The dizziness had abated, but a deep throb kept up a syncopated rhythm on the side of my head. I would have to remember to ask Gage Brewer about it. I wasn't all that hungry; the cats were. I fed them and then took some aspirin with a couple of cups of coffee.

It was a beautiful sunny day, very little wind by mid-morning. I had a yearn to roam, take in the city, breathe, and feel alive. Given all she had been through, I'm sure Debra Rose Nathan felt the same way, and I was on my way to find out.

Along with Donald Long, the young girl and her mother had just finished breakfast when I knocked at the door. It was open, the screen door identifying me as a welcome guest. I accepted the offer of more coffee. I figured it could only help my head.

After breakfast, Debra Rose tentatively related to me the horrifying experience. While she had been classmates with Jeremy Thatcher and knew him to say hello, she certainly wasn't close to him in any fashion and never had any intention of going to the prom with him. Just a delusion in his mind, an obsession she knew nothing about until it became too late.

"He said he wanted to show me a special collection. I figured if I didn't at least see what he was talking about he'd never leave me alone. I didn't think much of it until I got there. The house was dark, quiet, and musty, as though the place itself was dead."

"What was the collection?"

"I never found out. He struck me from behind and before I knew it, I was in that chair in the basement. He would feed me and give me water but said I was part of the house now. I guess I was the collection."

My experiences in the war showed me signs of human nature I had not dreamed of before. Now, with this tale, it was even worse than I imagined. I confirmed she had taken a roll of film from one of her sessions with Brooks Mellon.

"What did you do with it, Debra Rose?"

"I threw it in the Arkansas River."

I smiled. Donald Long noticed my expression.

"What's funny, Mr. Bergman?"

"*Tashlich*." His look went from concerned to perplexed. I referenced a ritual not of their world. "On the afternoon of the first day of Rosh Hashanah, the Jewish New Year, we say a prayer and symbolically throw our sins into a body of water. It is a ritual of repentance."

"I'm not Jewish," Debra Rose declared innocently. "Does it mean the same for me?"

I took her soft hands in mine and held back my tears. I knew she would be okay with all the love around her.

"*Chazak u'varuch*. Be strong and be blessed."

I nodded in the direction of Arlene Nathan, touched Debra Rose's cheek, and left this peaceful abode. Donald Long quickly followed me out.

"We can't thank you enough, Mr. Bergman. I don't know how we'll ever repay you."

I looked back at the meager home, considered the family inside, and saw the blessing of a restoration. That was payment enough.

"No. There is no need," I told Donald Long. "Besides, Uncle Sam has taken care of me well enough."

He didn't fully understand my meaning. I could see he desperately tried to offer me a token by way of recompense.

"I suppose you still wonder why I left music."

"No, Don, I don't. I've learned it is more important to let a man live his life. A whole bunch of folks think you might be better off in one direction or the other, and they might be right. But until you figure it out for yourself, everything is all just a guess." He smiled and nodded. "May I ask you a question?"

"Certainly."

"Do you have a good life?"

"Yes, sir." He looked back toward the house and then faced me. "Yes, I do."

"Well, then. That is all that really matters."

I patted him on the shoulder and left them to the glory of the day and beyond.

A quick mental calculation put me at ease about my financial state. I'd received twelve hundred and fifty dollars from Farmers and Bankers Life Insurance and half of the five grand gratuity, so to speak, from the FBI. It was time to start doling it out.

When I walked into Hebrew Congregation, I saw Rabbi Saperstein on the bimah with a younger man all dressed in the garb of a rebbe. Rabbi Saperstein faced in my direction, so I instinctively waved.

At that point, the younger man leaned in to whisper into the rabbi's ear. A wave of his arm welcomed me to join them.

As I approached, I could only assume Rabbi

Saperstein's vision had grown worse in such a brief time. He had told me not to be upset with his condition, but I couldn't help it. I still had to learn how to grasp Faith beyond all else.

"Harold, allow me to introduce to you Rabbi Yaakov Mendel of Lublin."

The man was relatively slender but had a firm handshake. A tall man, perhaps close to six feet. Though he may have been on this side of forty, just enough gray in his hair gave him both a scholarly as well as tired appearance. I sensed a noticeable calm to his presence, a kind of stillness that came across in his eyes and the delicate tenderness in his hands.

"Rabbi Saperstein has told me much of you and your father, Mr. Bergman, and of your heroism in the war."

"Perhaps not nearly as heroic as your efforts, Rabbi Mendel."

Most of the Jewish population of Lublin were deported to the Belzec concentration camp or exterminated in the Mejdanek concentration camp right outside the city. I had inferred he had suffered many unspeakable evils. His very presence here was testament to faith and strength. Like Debra Rose Nathan, we can always find the impulse deep within us that wants to live, that spark of meaning that gives our lives purpose.

Rabbi Saperstein reiterated his condition worsened, but they were pleased to have Rabbi Mendel take over shabbat and holiday services until the temple elders could find a permanent replacement.

Rabbi Mendel's blue-gray eyes had a sense of hope within them. He drew me to him as though he were the sunrise at dawn.

"We shall share tales of heroism and faith," he said

proudly.

"I look forward to that."

I shook his hand warmly and hugged Rabbi Saperstein. I placed an envelope in his hand.

"What is this, young Bergman?"

"For the temple. For your work."

Once again, I turned and left a house to the glory of the day and the joy of tomorrow.

Tyler Schenkel greedily stuffed his face with fried eggs and potatoes, bacon, and toast, slurped coffee to wash it all down, as manic as Woody Woodpecker. No one sat on either side of him at the counter of the Red Apple. That is, until I did.

"Them Army boys think they're tough," he grumbled.

"They are."

"Not as tough as me."

Just like a pig in a trough. I let him go on for a bit.

"When did they let you out?" I asked.

"Shortly after midnight. Good thing they left town already."

"Or?"

He shrugged his shoulders. The act was for anyone in earshot. He knew it didn't impress me much. I slid four twenties across the counter.

"What's this?" he asked, genuinely uncertain as to the monetary meaning, despite the greed in his eyes.

"I hired you. Remember?"

He used two fingers to count the bills right there on the counter, then went back to his meal.

"You're pretty generous."

"So I've been told."

I started to leave, but he called after me.

"Hey, how do you manage so well?"

I knew what he meant. We had both been in the war and seen things that small town guys like us would have never seen in a normal lifetime. It made it difficult for a whole bunch of us to get back to the life we had before. Tyler had opted for crime as an expression of his anger and frustration. I, apparently, was different, seeking an alternate path.

"I'm still trying to figure that out, Tyler."

After these two payments, I still had over thirty-one hundred dollars, enough for me to contemplate life as it stood right now. On Monday, I would pay my rent several months in advance to what I felt certain would be Mrs. Hanover's glee and deposit the rest in the bank.

I knew the bartender at the Kala Club up on North Market and stopped by to pick up a bottle of wine that he said a lady would like. My only experience was Manischewitz in temple. I declined an offer of whiskey as it didn't seem appropriate. I purchased my groceries on the way home at the Dillons on Thirteenth and Waco. My mother was a great cook, and I made sure to pay attention to what she did. There were never any recipes written down. She just knew what to do. She had that gift. Now, all I had to do was remember.

I soaked a couple of slices of bread in milk and then mixed it with ground beef, peas, and diced onion. I drizzled some catsup on top. Then, I cut a large potato into small cubes and placed it around the meatloaf. I toasted a few slices of challah. I put some cream cheese and a small piece of lox on each, placed them on the only decent serving dish I had, and kept it in the fridge. Since I was not a baker, I was fortunate to have the almond cookies from Mrs. Hanover to offer for dessert. My goal was to impress with intentions more than culinary skill. I had an abundance of the first over the latter.

Eileen arrived promptly at seven. She had met Lady Mittens and Sir Pounce before but was thoroughly taken with them as they were with her. She seemed at ease in my small apartment while I suddenly started to feel uncomfortable. She likely could sense my need to relax and accepted a glass of wine as I took out the appetizers.

"So, don't get me wrong," she started, "because I think all of this is lovely. But having you cook dinner is the last thing I ever expected."

"Maybe I'm branching out. Or maybe I'm just trying to feel human again."

"Been pretty difficult, huh?"

"Nothing is the same as it was before the war. And, by the same token, I feel rejuvenated by my work as a private investigator. I've learned about myself at the same time I rediscovered humanity."

Sir Pounce interrupted this quiet introspective moment when he jumped into Eileen's lap and nearly knocked over her plate.

"Have they been fed?" she asked.

"Yes."

We laughed. Sir Pounce was confused. Lady Mittens was noncommittal.

It thrilled me beyond measure to take out the baking dish and see that the meatloaf and potatoes looked palatable. I sliced up two large hunks, scooped out some potatoes, and tilted the dish enough to get the meat drippings as a kind of gravy. I put her plate in front of her, poured more wine, and then sat down. I had just about started to eat when she cleared her throat.

"I thought you usually said a prayer when you have

dinner with your father."

"Well, yeah." I clasped my head and bowed. "*Barukh atah Adonai Eloheinu, Melekh ha'olam, shehakol nih'ye bidvaro.*"

"Blessed art Thou, Lord our God, King of the universe, at Whose word all came to be. Amen."

"Amen," I responded.

My eyes darted up occasionally while we ate. I didn't wonder whether Eileen enjoyed herself. I simply saw her differently than I ever had before. We were friends in school. As young adults, we went in separate directions, largely because I might not have been an ideal suitor. We drew closer over the last few weeks.

My life was small at my choosing. I had the mistaken notion that I could keep it simple. However, my line of work made that almost an impossibility. What is it that I wanted? Perhaps it was right here in front of me.

"So, Harold, have you ever thought about having children?"

I smiled warmly, never answering her that I had.

A word about the author...

I studied film-making and creative writing at the University of Miami in the 80's, was involved in the Boston Poetry Scene in the 90's, and am a former president of the Kansas Writer's Association. My work has stretched from crime fiction to poetry, screen writing to experimental fiction. I am also co-host of Tikiman and The Viking podcast
https://open.spotify.com/show/5R3wY5THZtBGI0 8JX7yJn7#_=_

I live in Wichita, KS with my wife, Shelia, and Sir Pounce Alot (the orange manx) and Lady Mittens (the tuxedo manx).

BLOG: http://tikiman1962.wordpress.com

http://tikiman1962.wordpress.com